A Poor Man's Supper

Jim Gulledge

Deer Hawk Publications

Dedication
This book is dedicated to the real Vancie
who taught me what the rooster says.

Acknowledgements

While writing this novel, I have been like a hen that could only lay an egg in the woods. The intensity of my job and home life have necessitated fleeing to the wilderness to make any real headway with this story. I extend my eternal thanks to Connie Furrer and Francis Dudley for founding the Snail's Pace Retreat House in Saluda, North Carolina, where I began this story, and to the many others who perpetuated their vision for over four decades. I also offer great thanks to Dr. Melicent Huneycutt-Vergeer, who first led me to Snail's Pace and taught me that I would never see the world completely until I saw it through myth, metaphor, archetype, and symbol, and to Shirley Boone, who started my writing habit with a single image of a frozen lake. My appreciation is also extended to the monks of Mepkin Abbey in Monks Corner, South Carolina who took me in on numerous occasions without once checking my credentials, spiritual or otherwise. More recently, I am indebted to Dale and Cindy Newport and Mike and Delaine Macdonald, who offered me use of their cabins on the Uwharrie and Nantahala Rivers for the completion of this tale. It was on the Uwharrie that Dr. Joseph Pate put me in a canoe and showed me the end of this book long before there was even a beginning.

After the initial manuscript was finished, I began the humbling process of realizing just how many people it takes with all of their wonderful and diverse talents to bring a book to its full flower. I am eternally indebted to Chelsea Weir, my editor, for her endless hours of work in editing my manuscript. In addition, I will never be able to begin to repay Aurelia Sands, my publisher, for believing in me and taking a chance on a middle-aged, unpublished writer. There's no way that I will ever understand all of the details that she has taken care of behind the scenes during a difficult period of her life to assure that this book would ever see the light of day. In its last stages, <u>A Poor Man's Supper</u> needed images as well as words. In those moments, God sent me Grainger McKoy and Josh Cross. Mr. McKoy generously granted permission of the use of his sketch for the cover of the book and Josh used his artistic skills to "frame" the sketch and create further connections to the text of the book.

My most heartfelt gratitude is reserved for my family. First, I give thanks for my paternal grandmother, whose soul enlivens each page. I also give thanks to my parents and siblings, who taught me love of the land and the meaning of family. As a person ages, there comes a time when a parent's thoughts turn to the legacy that will be left for their children. I have been driven by a desire to share what I know of life in this tale; so, Megan, Adam, Jenna, and Gillian, in these few pages are all that I know of life in this world. I wish you well in your own discoveries.

Finally, my greatest thanks are reserved for my wife, Linda, and the Giver of all good things who brought her to me. Without you and your constant encouragement and affirmation, this story would never have been started or finished and the story of my life would have lacked its greatest riches.

Prologue

A red-tailed hawk rose on the currents of the afternoon thermals, gliding around and around the crown of the weather-beaten pine before resting on an outstretched branch. From his perch, the bird looked out upon the vista that stretched before his keen eyes. Below him, a rustle in the grass turned his attention from the heavens to the earth. A small cottontail emerged from its hiding and nibbled at wildflowers on the edge of the cliff. Before the hawk could muster its instincts to respond, another motion entered the scene just below the rabbit. The head of an Eastern diamondback rattlesnake emerged over the rim of the ravine and flattened out as it wound closer to its prey. The rabbit saw nothing and knew nothing until it felt a flash, the sensation of warm fluid oozing into its cranium, and the stiffening of limbs and darkening of senses. The snake coiled in bliss around the twitching ball of fur and fluids.

Its revelry, however, was short-lived. In another flash, a convulsion of pain interrupted the snake's pleasure as sharp talons penetrated its flesh and lifted it skyward. Soon, the hawk sat upon his perch once again and tore the eyes from the motionless serpent. Had the bird cared to notice at that moment, a man descended from the peaks above and another wound his way up the rugged escarpment below. The blood lettings of men were about to play out again beneath the watchful eyes of the bird, but hawks are creatures of the air and take no notice of the affairs of men. That he would leave to the one who made them. Slowly, the raptor lifted and again rode the warm afternoon breezes, oblivious to all hungers but its own.

Chapter One
Vancie Keller

Vancie Keller rocked slowly back and forth on the weather-worn porch of the farm house. She looked the part of an expensive, French, store-bought doll, and she was as uncomfortable as hell. Mattie had spent all day Friday boiling her clothes in the big wash pot in the backyard and most of the day on Saturday pressing them with a hot iron. The end result was clothes with creases so sharp that they threatened to draw blood every time that Vancie turned. After all of her dancing around, Mattie had finally threatened her life.

"Child if you twist yourself one more time, it ain't your starched-up dress that is going to hurt you."

Her mother, Lois, had worked her body over in the same fashion in a washtub in the summer kitchen, scrubbing her until Vancie was sure that she would bleed. It was Sunday morning now, and Vancie had been parked on the front porch, hair curled, with instructions to rock just fast enough to fan but not fast enough to sweat. Her only hope of salvation was Big John pulling the wagon around front, loading her sorry self into it, and getting up enough speed for her to at least feel the spring breeze blowing through her hair on the way to another form of torture: church.

Sadly, Vancie was about the only pretty thing on the Keller farm that morning with the exception of some buttercups blooming by the front steps. Although her family's farm had once been a showplace in the small, mountain community, life had not been kind to the Kellers. Vancie's dad had come back from the war briefly, but not in one piece. With part of his left leg gone, and even more of his mind, Marcus Keller was never a real farmer again before his death. God knows he tried. Big John and Mattie tried even harder, but injury and age had left their mark on the Keller place. Even deeper than the gullies in the field were Lois Keller's facial lines. Though she was once a woman of exceptional beauty, her husband's death and her family's unrelenting slide toward poverty left wounds on Lois's body and soul. All the brightness of her youth had vanished, to be replaced by a sharp tongue and dark disposition.

Every time Vancie made a false step, her mother's words pelted her like hail in a summer storm.

"Go ahead then, you fool child. You're more and more like your daddy every day. Always off in a dream. Well, dreams won't fill your belly, and honor and nobility don't satisfy the bank. You need to get some sense. Look where his noble dreams got him! Life is hard, and it's all about surviving in a tough world. Instead of looking for a man to come along with a buggy load of fancies, you had better be looking for a man to come your way with a pocket full of silver!"

Vancie had heard this speech more times than she had seen lightning bugs in the yard. Fact was, she just didn't care. She hardly ever thought about men and never thought about the considerable beauty she had inherited from her mother. The only time that Vancie Keller ever saw her own face was on a clear day when she was looking in the creek water for tadpoles. She would rather be wrapped in barbed wire than strapped into a church dress with her cheeks pinched and her body scented with rosewater. As soon as their wagon pulled back into the yard after church and dinner on the grounds, she would drop her dress on the floor of her room, pull on her britches, and be out the back door to save what was left of the day exploring the woods, creeks, and meadows on the farm.

"Well," Vancie shouted to her mama while she was going out the back door, "if I ever find a man, he'll have to be standing in the middle of a creek!"

Chapter Two
Josiah Buckland

Josiah Buckland's coarse, homespun clothes chafed against the sharp angles of his sixteen-year-old frame as he strode down the middle of the road into Tugaloo. He wasn't alone as he rounded the last curve of the twisting mountain road and came into sight of Main Street. A disheveled and noticeably hungover farmer drove a small band of brown, mud-caked pigs into town about twenty yards in front of him. As he struck the ones bringing up the rear, grunts and squeals joined the growing cacophony of sound of the town on a market day. Josiah felt his insides rear back in revulsion as he was enveloped by the whinnying of horses, the slap of leather reins, shouts of merchants loading and unloading goods, and the squeals of raga-muffin children come to town on their once-a-week pilgrimage.

Sound wasn't the only thing that assaulted Josiah's forest-honed senses. After a late rain last night, the main boulevard of Tugaloo had become a festering cesspool of mud, tobacco juice, pig urine, horse shit and flies. His deer skin shoes soon reeked with corruption as he labored to suck one and then another up from the fetid muck that passed as a street in Tugaloo. Only necessity and survival had driven Josiah down the mountain. He longed for the silence and solace of massive fir trees, impenetrable rhododendron thickets, and sunlit mountain balds; but some evil, or a series of them, had come to the high country in recent years.

Loggers clear cut entire ridges and other lowlanders burned off meadows, hoping to coax crops from the rocky, thin soil of the mountaintops. Somehow, in their coming, they had brought a plague to the great trees of the Blue Ridge and Smokies. The massive giants that provided wood for cabins, farm tools, furniture, and forage for black bears and deer were dying off by the tens of thousands. The whole food chain of the high country had been undone. Once-prosperous settlements and game lands now offered up little to those who clung to their wasting remains for sustenance. His parents had passed with the passing of the great trees, so Josiah had been driven by hunger and loneliness to the lower altitude of Tugaloo.

The buildings of the town were aligned in an odd quarter circle arc the length of Main Street. At first sight, it looked like the street had been laid out by a moonshiner rather than a surveyor. However, after staring for a few moments, the logic of the street slowly revealed itself to Josiah. The timbered storefronts of the street had been built to mimic the serpentine arc of the older road and the newly laid tracks of the rails of the Piedmont-Blue Ridge Railroad.

The rail line to Tugaloo was a marvel of engineering that climbed nearly twenty-five hundred feet out of the Piedmont on the steepest grade in the Appalachian Mountains. Dozens of men had died making it as they routed the railway up the ancient Stairway to Heaven trading path of the Cherokee. Others had perished in its initial runs when train engineers lost their battles with the forces of nature as the behemoth iron horses tried to descend back to the lowlands overloaded with timber and other booty from the high country. Josiah found himself wishing that the town folk would all die as a locomotive stalled at the depot released a hiss and scream of wood-fueled vapor into the already unnerving racket of the town. For a few moments, pandemonium ensued as mountain horses, unused to the dawning age of steam and metal, reared onto their hind legs. Pigs scattered, chickens took flight, and wide-eyed children shrieked in response. It was more than Josiah could take. He fled up a side alley and into the sanctuary of the old livery stable a block away from the chaos.

Once inside the livery, sanity returned. The buildings of Main Street and the angle of the alley somehow absorbed the noisy chaos. Josiah breathed in the sweetness of newly-mown hay and the muskiness of placid beasts chewing their cud in silence. He had never known until coming to town that silence was the essence and necessity of his life. He had always taken it for granted, like the sky, wind, spring water, and the earth itself. Josiah found himself never wishing to leave the livery again.

"Well, if I have to live in this hellhole, maybe I can find some work here. Everybody has to take care of their horse," mused the boy.

Josiah, walked through the silent, cathedral-like passage of the ancient barn and eventually found a doorway to a lean-to addition out back. He softly rapped on the dilapidated doorway, afraid that it was as likely that some form of vermin would emerge as it was a human might appear. However, after another knock or two, Josiah heard the latch lift and stepped back as the door swung inward on its rusty hinges, scraping against the frame. Josiah gasped in surprise and suppressed his impulse to laugh at what stood before him. By the color of his remaining hair, beard, and sideburns, the man in the doorway seemed to be in his late forties to early fifties. However, by his stature, he appeared little more than a boy in his early teens. To call him a dwarf would have been a little less than the truth, but not by much. At full attention, the man standing on the stoop could be no more than five feet tall. Although he was barrel-chested, other signs of physical weakness prevailed. He had a small pair of square-lens spectacles perched on the end of his nose, and as he took a step closer, Josiah noticed that his right foot was twisted to the side, producing a pronounced limp.

"Hello, my name is Phineus Coble. I run the livery here in Tugaloo. What can I do for you, boy?"

Josiah struggled to imagine the man-child before him wrangling horses in and out of the stalls of the livery or feeding or shoeing them, but suddenly he snapped out of his reverie and answered, "Mr. Phineus, I am Josiah Bunyan Buckland, and I need myself a job. Things have gotten hard up in the high country, and I have come to town looking for me some work. Do you have any jobs for me?"

Phineus looked the boy up and down, sizing him up on the outside against a hard day's labor, but then he looked up into Josiah's eyes. Phineus's father had always told him that when doing business with a man, his eyes were the windows of truth. If that was the case, Josiah Buckland's eyes were the windows to heaven itself. In most other ways, the boy was ordinary: tall, angular-framed, with thick, brown hair hanging nearly to his shoulders. Everything about his body was of the earth. In fact, Josiah's body seemed somehow an incarnation of soil, tree, and rock. But not his eyes. When Josiah straightened to full height and his hair fell back from his face, it revealed two of the most startling eyes that Phineus Coble had ever seen. Sometimes when people stood at the right angle at the right time of day, the sky was partly reflected in the orbs of their eyes. However, Josiah's eyes did not reflect the sky. They seemed to be the sky itself; at times nearly gray, and at others, dark sapphire, like the sky in the mountains before the sudden crash of thunder and fall of rain.

Though Phineus was poor as a church mouse himself, he suddenly heard himself agreeing to give the boy shelter and meager rations in exchange for six days a week of hard labor. He couldn't decide if his actions constituted charity or abuse on his own part, but his words were spoken before he knew that they had formed in his head. The reaction on Josiah's part was one of pure delight. Tonight, he wouldn't sleep in the rain. He wouldn't struggle to sleep over the rumblings of his empty stomach.

"Thank you, Mr. Phineus. Thank you, Sir." the boy replied respectfully over and over again as he shook the tiny man's hand who smiled before him.

Chapter Three
The Meeting

Josiah Buckland worked feverishly at the livery stable, fueled by the deep, abiding gratitude he felt for Phineus Coble. Mr. Phineus had taken him in when he was hungry, put a meal in his belly and a roof over his head that night. In the weeks since then, their relationship had progressed from one of employer and laborer to one more closely approximating father and son. Although Josiah enjoyed the kind of care which he had not received since the passing of his own father, it was still difficult to accept Mr. Phineus's kindness. Josiah intended to earn his keep with his sweat. Every day, he rose early while the moon still hung in the sky and long before the roosters, scattered around town, heralded the dawning of day. He set to work mucking out stalls, scattering oats in the feeding troughs, and hauling bucket after bucket of water from the old communal well at the end of Black Rock Road.

Unfortunately, when the sun finally rose, it flamed with a vengeance. Summer pressed down upon Tugaloo as the day brightened. The cool night air dissipated quickly and was replaced by the creeping humidity of

July. It would be a long, sweltering day. A hay wagon had been pulled into the barn the night before and it was Josiah's job to lift the contents, pitchfork by pitchfork, from the bed of the large wagon to the loft high above. The walls of the barn, which had sheltered him from the night just hours before, now worked against him as they closed out the breaths of air that occasionally stirred around the wooden structures on Main Street. Within a few hours, the dampness of the air clung to his skin and coalesced into droplets which, by noon, merged into rivulets that streamed down his back, chest, arms, and legs.

Each time Josiah pitched a new forkful of hay into the loft, straw dust and bits of chaff rained downward clinging to his wet shirt, collecting in his hair, invading his nostrils, and joining the already stinging sweat in his eyes. He peeled his shirt over his head, swiped his arm across his brow, and kept going. There was no point counting the strokes of his arm lifting the hay upward. Day would have slipped away before the last forkful of the dried grass lay safely in the loft. His only duty was to stoop, scoop, pitch, and blink as the debris continued to rain down upon him.

Dinner, when it came from Mr. Phineus, was simple, but ample: a few slices of cheese and a hunk of bread. Water was drawn in a dipper from one of the buckets carried in for the horses. It was no different than what Phineus Coble ate at noon today. Mr. Coble lived the life of a pauper. The only luxury that Josiah had ever seen the little man indulge himself was a tin penny whistle, which the boy would sometimes hear him play late in the evening.

Supper would be much the same as dinner with beans instead of bread, but his stomach would not ache from emptiness as it had the many days and nights in the woods on his way down the mountain trails from the highlands. Unless Mr. Phineus dropped by during the day or a customer delivered or retrieved a horse, the only voices Josiah would hear were those of the barn swallows as they darted in and out of the opening at the front of the structure.

Josiah settled into the rhythm of his work and comforted himself with his awareness of his growing strength. As the weeks passed, he felt the tightening of the sinews in his arms, legs, back, and chest. Though far from manhood, he smiled at the thought of the recent crackling of his voice and the emergence of small patches of hair under his arms, about his face, and around his cock. Most mornings when he rose, his cock had risen before him in small imitation of its far larger, more intimidating counterparts dangling from the stallions in the barn. At first, these changes had startled him, but now, he found them strangely comforting. He had had to play the part of a man for a long time now, it was nice to finally be growing into it.

"Hello, Boy," said a small, sweet voice behind him.

Josiah nearly threw his pitchfork into the loft with the hay. Heart pounding, he wheeled around on the balls of his feet and faced a girl standing nearly nose-to-chest behind him.

"What are you trying to do, you little fool, kill me?" Josiah yelled.

But as she lifted her face up to him, Josiah suddenly found himself lost in the blueness of her eyes. He felt at home again, back in the safety and beauty of the forests in the upper reaches of the mountain summits. The coolness of her breath invaded his space, sweetened the rankness of his own odor, and awakened him from the numbness of work.

As his senses cleared, he became aware of his half-nakedness, ripped his shirt from the fencepost, and pulled the soiled cloth over his damp body. In a panic, he realized that she had awakened more than his sensibilities, so he dropped the tail of the thick, coarse material down rather than tucking it in.

"Are you here to pick up a horse or something?" he stammered.

Her eyes sparkled with delight, and she laughed musically.

"Why, you silly boy, do I look like a customer at a livery stable? I was just walking into town to the mercantile and saw you in here trying to bury yourself in a pile of hay with a pitchfork."

Josiah blushed crimson, half in embarrassment and half in rage.

"So I guess you could do a better job yourself, Girl, in your little calico dress?" he retorted.

"Well, the only thing that I'm sure of is that I couldn't possibly do a worse one," the girl fired back.

Lightning flashed in Josiah's eyes, but even as he felt his heart pounding, he was aware of a great lie. He heard the anger and sarcasm in his voice and felt the pounding in his temples, but inside, he knew he could stand anything that she might say to him as long as she continued to speak. The only thing that he couldn't stand was to never hear her voice again and never fall into her eyes again.

At that very moment, to his horror, she turned around, tossed her golden hair behind her, and sashayed out of the barn, calling out behind her, "My name is Vancie Keller, and you can tuck your shirt in now."

Josiah Buckland stood lost in a wave of rage, shame, and longing.

As Josiah stood in the doorway of the livery looking sadly down the now empty street, a small, sharp voice behind him shocked him back to his senses.

"So, is this why I provide you with room and board, for you to moon around staring off into space after I've given you a job to do?" barked his employer.

"Oh, I'm so sorry, Mr. Phineus. I'll get right back to work, sir," Josiah answered apologetically.

"What's wrong with you today, Boy? Lollygagging around isn't like you. Are you feeling sickly today?"

Josiah was tempted to simply grab his pitchfork and return to his labors, but to his own surprise, he began to pour out his heart to the small, bespectacled man. "Mr. Phineus, I met a girl. Not just any girl, mind you, I am certain that I met *the* girl, the girl that I will spend the rest of my days with, the girl that'll bear my children and love me forever."

Phineus Coble was tempted to mock the excesses of youth, but something in the pain on the boy's face and the vulnerability in his eyes stopped him. Josiah Buckland stood before him, his heart exposed without defense. The wrong word would pierce him like an arrow and poison him with the seed of adult cynicism forever. A wound from Phineus's own youth rose up inside of him, constricting his vocal chords. He knew that a boy could meet a girl and love her forever, and he knew the pain that endured when she didn't return the favor. The words that finally came to Phineus were not of his own making.

"What's her name, Josiah?"

"Her name is Vancie, Sir."

Two weeks later at dinner, Phineus, with mist in his eyes, approached Josiah at the table, took his right hand, and pressed a small round object into it. Josiah peeled back his fingers and gasped in surprise.

"Why, Mr. Phineus. It's gold!"

A small, rose-colored lady's pocket watch, no larger than a dollar, lay in Josiah's calloused hand.

"Where did you get this, Sir? No offense, but you're poor. How did you afford something like this, and why are you giving it to me?"

Phineus Coble pulled back the small chair beside of him and took a seat, his feet dangling above the dusty floor.

"Josiah, it's too late for me. The feelings that you have for Vancie were there for me, too, for a girl of my own when I was a boy. However, there are people in this world for whom love will never be more than feelings, small people, crippled people, poor people. I'm getting old now. There will never be a girl for me, and there will never be children of my own to whom I can pass my mother's wedding watch. You're as close to a son as I will ever have. I did a reckless thing last week. Look, there's a small clasp on the watch. Press it and open the back cover."

Josiah followed Phineus's instructtions, prying open the slightly dented back of the watch. Newly etched on the inside of the back cover of the watch, Josiah found the initials: *V. K. and J. B.* "Mr. Phineus, it's our initials. You ruined your mother's watch!"

"Well, ruined is perhaps a bit harsh. I guess if worst came to worst, the letters could be scratched off, but something in my heart tells me that that won't be necessary. Call it a leap of faith if you wish. A leap of faith in the young and in the mystery of things. You're worth the risk."

Josiah looked at the small man before him and realized that there are debts in life which cannot be repaid. Laying his large hand on the top of Phineus Coble's diminutive one, Josiah realized that he now owed such a debt.

Phineus looked him squarely in the eyes and said, "And forget any nonsense about paying me back. Just pick up some nails for me at the hardware tomorrow and we'll call it even."

21

Chapter Four
The Stars

Josiah plodded along the road out of Tugaloo. Although the livery provided some buffer from the smells and noises of town, at least once a week, he simply had to leave. Most people would fear walking out of the comfort and security of community and into the terrors of the night, but with each step away from the lights of town, Josiah felt the tightness in his body and the oppression of his heart lift. For a woodsman on an exposed road without a tree canopy, it wasn't even particularly dark. Josiah's eyes had long ago become accustomed to the soft light of stars, and it was all that he needed to lengthen his stride and quicken his pace as he left the clamor of town in the distance.

Soon, the only sounds surrounding him were those that cleared his senses: the murmur of a small stream running along the road bed, the incessant chirps of crickets, and the plaintive call of the whip-poor-will. The air cooled. An occasional cloud blocked out patches of the stars that streamed like dia-monds across the heavens. All was now well as Josiah sank into a state of peace, solitude, and healing. Another mile or so down the road, Josiah heard the soft strains of singing and tensed at the prospect of encountering someone on his walk. For a moment, he thought of plunging into the darkness of the forest to avoid human contact.

He paused and saw movement to his right in a small meadow. Darting about in the glade, spinning madly like a whirling dervish, a girl came into focus. With the light of the stars upon her, she appeared to be dressed in the palest white. He could barely see a ringlet of small meadow flowers against her golden hair in the dimness of the night. As she ran and danced, she sang in a clear soprano voice like a nightingale:

Star light, star bright,
The first star I have seen tonight;
I wish I may, I wish I might,
Have the wish I have wished tonight.

Each time she uttered the lines, she burst into waves of joyful laughter and spun about beneath the glow of the Pleiades. Josiah stopped dead in his tracks, in love with the flower-crowned nymph twirling wildly through the night. At that moment, the forest above the field appeared to burst into flame. Josiah shrank back in terror until he realized that the glow wasn't fire, but the full crimson moon rising above the ridge of the hill.

Before he knew what he was doing, he dashed from the road, across the small stream, and out into the field. Seeing him in pursuit, the girl fled like a deer before hounds.

Josiah followed as the moon slowly turned orange, then yellow, and finally white, illuminating everything in sight nearly to the brightness of day. However, before Josiah could catch his prey, she leapt from the bright meadow into the darkness of the forest with him just yards behind. Even for a seasoned woodsman, Josiah found the darkness of the forest temporarily disorienting, but his eyes quickly adjusted. He caught a glimpse of her receding figure and took off after her.

After chasing her for what seemed like miles, he suddenly cried out in despair, "Stop! Come back!" His voice echoed through the forest. Only silence returned to him. He had lost her.

He felt his chest heave, his legs burn, and his heart ache with emptiness and loss. As he turned to leave in defeat, something happened which he had only seen one other time in his life. Fireflies suddenly illuminated the darkness, but not as they do most places. In most places, fireflies pulsate in scattered, twinkling succession. However, in a few magical places in the mountains, they all spark in perfect synchronization. The effect was startling. The woods vacillated from inky blackness to stardust illumination, like a lamp turned nearly to nothing and then up again to full flame. As the fireflies lighted, he saw her no more than twenty feet away. He stepped forward. Darkness fell. Then the fires flared again. Each time they did, Josiah found himself closer to the god-child. In darkness, his hand found hers and pulled her body close. In warm light, she lifted her head toward him. In darkness, he kissed her soft, moist lips, and in a flash of light he knew her to be not a goddess, but the girl that he had met at the livery a few weeks before. As their lips parted, Josiah reached to the depths of his trouser pocket, retrieved the cold, golden circle of the watch, and pressed it into her small hand. Vancie smiled faintly, tightened her hand around it, pulled away, and bolted into the night. Her form grew ever smaller and dimmer as she retreated.

Chapter Five
Jagger Hill

Jagger Hill stepped lightly down from the passenger compartment of the train. A cloud of steam enveloped him as the engine belched its last breaths after the long struggle up the mountainside. Once the vapors cleared, Jagger got his first glimpse of Tugaloo in its workday squalor. His attraction to Tugaloo wasn't to what it was, but to what it might become with his help. He had spent months poring over maps of the southeast, looking for a small town poised for the opportunity of explosive growth and great wealth. Tugaloo was the winner.

Although it was little more than a pig path now, the coming railroad would make the village the first point of arrival for goods exchanged between the high country and low country. Jagger knew opportunity when he saw it, and he saw opportunity in Tugaloo. Unlike so many other men, he didn't place all his faith for success in his intellect and unbridled drive. Jagger held his ace in the hole in the leather bag dangling from his left hand. He had possessed his wealth for nearly twenty years, so long, in fact, that a few good turns had swelled his initial fortune. The years had, however, also clouded Jagger's memories of its origins. He had affected the role of a gentleman for so long and spun so many stories about the blueness of his blood that even he had begun to believe them. The real source of Jagger's wealth lay deeply hidden within the sheltered recesses of his own mind and heart; hidden from all he met, and hidden after all these years even from himself.

Jagger had forgotten many things. He'd forgotten the hardscrabble life of his boyhood, working on a rock-strewn farm, chopping cotton by day and being beaten by his foul-mouthed immigrant father at night. He'd forgotten the idealistic young man who marched off to defend the honor of Dixie in exchange for escaping the rot of his childhood. Most of all, Jagger had forgotten Robert Laurens.

He had met Robert early in the war and was immediately drawn to him. The Laurens had the life that Jagger longed for when his stomach twisted with hunger in the fields. Colonial blue-bloods, the Laurens had built upon their privilege and nobility by erecting one of the finest plantation houses in the low country. That did them little good as the tide of the war turned unrelentingly against the South. The grand palace, populated now by women, Robert's own sickly, pasty-faced child, and a few remaining negroes, stood trembling on the brink of extinction.

Terror about the fate of his family and several near misses on the battlefield had caused Robert to lose faith, and, in a moment of weakness, he had poured out his sorrows.

"Jagger, you're my best friend. Promise me. Please, promise me. If we fail; if I die and you live, promise me that you'll go back to Penland. I have a secret there. A way for my family and you to survive after the war. There are crypts behind the main house in the woods, crypts of all of the Laurens who ever lived at Penland. In my grandfather, Henry's, crypt, there is gold. Lots of gold. Enough for all of you to survive and start a new life. I didn't even tell Lucy. Promise me if anything happens that you'll save them."

Jagger did make a promise that night. Thirteen days later, Robert Laurens died mid-morning from a rifle ball to the head. In the confusion of battle, it escaped the notice of all survivors that the ball had entered the back of Robert's head and exited between his eyes.

Jagger kept his promise after the war and went to Penland. However, the few malnourished, diseased occupants who re-mained were never aware of his visit. He came in the night and only paid his respects to Robert Lauren's grandfather. If he ever justified anything that he did, it was that nobility had proven itself unworthy. The victor of war was the survivor, and to the survivor went the spoils. Jagger Hill was a survivor.

Jagger strode confidently down the wooden walkways of Tugaloo, a town he knew he would soon own. Tipping his hat to the younger ladies passing by, he surveyed the town, taking inventory of each building, wagon, and person; sorting what he might keep from what he would not. Suddenly, Jagger grasped for a porch post, struggling to keep his equilibrium as a dirty, brown-haired street urchin careened into him at full speed.

Regaining his footing, Jagger grabbed the youth by the nape of the neck and spat invectives at him while he took the boy's hair in his other hand and jerked his head backward. Jagger Hill stared down into the lad's eyes with shock and revulsion. Two grayish-blue orbs pierced him like spears. Suddenly, Jagger felt like he would fall into their depths and be consumed. He jolted back in horror at the sensation.

The boy looking up at the man experienced a terror of his own. Every survival instinct brought Josiah to full alertness. Josiah had the disturbing sensation that the face that he looked at was not the real face of the man. His real face lurked somewhere deep behind the outer mask of the man. Josiah shivered, jerked himself free from Jagger's grasp, and lunged backward.

Babbling, he said, "I'm sorry. I was just on my way to the hardware to get some nails for my boss. Please forgive me for being careless."

Then, he bolted down the boardwalk. Jagger quickly composed himself, adjusted his clothes, and promptly buried any memory of the encounter with the youth as deeply as possible in his psyche. Jagger Hill had no desire or capacity to retain any experience with a young hoodlum who had somehow made him feel less of a man.

Chapter Six
The Falls

Vancie carefully forced her way through the thickets of rhododendron and laurel along the banks of Colt Creek. Occasionally, the ground cover was so dense she had no other choice than to take to the waters of the stream, gingerly jumping from rock to rock as she slowly worked her way closer to the falls. At times, she got discouraged by the excruciating pace of her journey, but soon found herself cheered by the increasing music of the waterfall. The walls of the holler closed in on both sides of the creek. Had it not been nearly noon, she would have already been shrouded in darkness. The sun only penetrated the depths of the gorge from late morning to early afternoon, but for now, the bright, golden rays warmed her shoulders to offset the iciness of the chilled water splashing over her bare feet. Like the brown trout hiding in the murky waters, she continued her struggle up the stream. Vancie heard few sounds other than her own breath and heartbeat, the cascading waters of the stream, and the occasional piping and warbling of the forest birds. As far as her senses could reveal at this moment, she was the only human being on Earth. This sensation continued unbroken until she rounded the last bend and saw Parson's Falls. The sight made Vancie catch her breath.

The sun rested at the top of the cataract, illuminating the water in a whiteness that stood out in blinding contrast to the emerald hues of the surrounding woodlands. As magnificent as this view was, that wasn't what had taken away the young girl's breath. At the foot of the three-tiered wall of water stood Josiah Buckland, the teenaged boy who she had encountered at the livery, and with whom she had cavorted under the stars. He had stripped off his clothes on the bank of the pool and now stood with his lean, muscled shoulders and taut buttocks facing her. He rinsed his shoulder-length blond hair in the foamy water, rotating his young body as the sun poured down through the white waters upon him. He stepped from the water, fully exposing his angular face, strong chest, long loins, and the dark encircling web around his fully-matured manhood. She should have been embarrassed and had been trained to know shame, but at that moment, she felt only the thrill of being in his presence without any of the artificial barriers that separated man from woman. She knew that it was a sin, but for a moment, she felt that she stood before some long ago and long-since-forgotten god of the forest and waters.

Paralyzed momentarily by surprise, Josiah stood statue-like before regaining his senses and wading out across the pool to reclaim his clothes. Vancie knew that she should retreat, but instead, found herself crossing the sandbar to him, ripe with well-intended, insincere apologies for her invasion of his privacy and dignity. Her advance caused Josiah to freeze again before her. Despite his embarrassment, he simply stopped and turned to her. Vancie watched enraptured as the last glistening drops of water slipped across the surfaces of his body and dripped down the tips of his fingers. She braced herself to laugh, cry, or scream, but no sound came. In sheer amazement of her own actions, her spirit rose from her body and watched her fingers wander to the straps of her cotton dress. Slowly, they twisted until the clasps opened, dropping her flower-patterned dress around her feet.

In some strange gesture of equilibrium within her irrational mind, she revealed herself to Josiah Buckland. The just ripening curvature of her hips and small, milky breasts stood exposed to the widening glare of his gray eyes. Her small belly stretched down to the auburn triangle of her own emerging identity as a woman. For several moments, they stood silently in a strange state of comfort before each other, no more self-conscious than the mares and stallions sharing quarters back at the livery. Josiah abandoned all pretense of retrieving his clothes as he stepped forward to sense Vancie more fully. She felt her nipples tighten into small, taut knots as he sniffed the sweetness of her hair and ran the edge of his fingernail across her neck from ear to shoulder. Josiah stepped back momentarily as he felt his stiffening phallus rise to close the small distance between them. At that mo- ment, Vancie felt the exhilaration of the dew at his tip, finding the moisture of her own body that had not come from the stream but from some place of mystery within her. She was overcome with desire and fell with him into the mossy bank of the stream.

Cascades of dripping water seeped from the banks of the small grotto and slipped over moss, leaf, and rock in rhythmic pro- fusion around them as their young bodies joined. The first human sound of the after- noon emerged from Vancie as a muffled cry erupted from her lips. However, the sensation of pain was followed by wave after wave of mounting warmth as Josiah pressed himself within her and began thrusting in an ever- increasing instinctive fury. The frantic bodies of the young lovers pressed more deeply into the mossy bank, and their fingernails pressed more desperately into the flesh of each other's shoulders until Josiah erupted within her. She felt herself transported in spasms of heat and muscular release. The young lovers lay panting together with lips separated, but their shoulders, nipples, hips, and genitals still locked in a moisture-dampened, slowly loosening union.

Josiah muttered, "You're like a dream from another world."

The words coming from his lips ran through Vancie like a lightning strike. As the last bit of Josiah slipped from her, he stood once again exposed to Vancie's full gaze. She stared in shock and despair. The orbs that moments ago had seemed egg-like were now small and tight against his frame, and his cock, rope-like before, now dangled nearly flush to the bottom of his torso. His once shining blond hair now hung ordinary, damp and brown upon his shoulders. Whatever spell had bewitched her faded like morning mist on a summer's day. The god-man, mighty and awe-inspiring, now revealed him-self as a tall, lean, awkward teen, scampering self-consciously around the beach, gathering his clothes and pressing them to his bare body.

"Why, you're only a boy!" Vancie blurted.

Instantly, she realized the wound her words caused, and wished to reach out and regather them to her mouth. The damage was immediate and deep. Josiah froze, blushed crimson, and desperately pulled at his tangled trousers until he had covered what remained of his badly mangled manhood. Vancie fled in embarrassment and shame.

Chapter Seven
Retreat

Vancie stumbled back down Colt Creek and ran the entire way to the Keller farm, trying to distance herself from the memory of lying with Josiah Buckland. What devil had possessed her to give herself away to a boy in the middle of the woods? What if Mama Lois found out? She would disown her and turn her out onto the road. Vancie stopped long enough to take a short bath in the creek on her mother's farm to wash the last vestiges of Josiah Buckland from her body and her mind before entering the house and falling under the piercing gazes of Mattie and her mother.

She had barely stepped onto the back porch when the first assault of words struck her like lighting from the kitchen.

"Where have you been, Girl? I thought I done told you to be out there weeding that garden before the briars and the brambles be the only thing we got left to eat. What you been up to with yourself?" Mattie spat, training her milky eyes to Vancie.

"I've just been down to the branch and lost track of the time." Vancie mumbled in reply.

"I expect that there be more to the story than that," Mattie fired back, "but I don't have no more of my time to waste today on a trifling girl. Get yourself to the dining room and set the table so I can get you and your mama some dinner before it get dark."

In disgust, Mattie turned back to the stove and her duties. Vancie bounded up the hall stairs, past her mother who was on the front porch shelling beans, and slipped into her room, closing the door tightly behind her.

Thank God, Mattie is half-blind, thought Vancie as she took off her mud-stained clothing and hid them under the bed. She would slip them into a boiling pot later in the week. Her nakedness made her self-conscious, so she quickly put on clean clothes and went downstairs to set the table and try to slide back into the ordinary routines of life on the Keller farm.

For a while, Vancie thought that she'd gotten away with her ruse. She immersed herself in her chores and carefully avoided any contact with town, especially the livery. However, several weeks after her encounter on Colt Creek, she got out of bed only to be overwhelmed by surges of intense nausea. Vancie barely had time to grab a chamber pot by her bed before she heaved last night's supper and successive waves of greenish yellow phlegm into the pot. She broke out in a cold sweat fearing that her gags had awakened her mother, but when her bedroom door squeaked open, things were worse than she had feared. Mattie stood with arms akimbo and feet planted firmly in the doorframe.

"Well, looks like baby girl may have lost more than the track of time in the woods," sighed Mattie sourly.

Within the hour, Mattie had delivered the bad news to the mistress of the house. Lois Keller sat in her porch rocker, teeth clenched, madder than a red wasp.

"Damn fool child, the spitting image of her weak-willed father. Well, Marcus Keller may not have done his duty in protecting this family from the sins of this world, but, by God, Lois Keller will not make the same mistake."

She wasn't about to let some stray mongrel destroy what was left of her family and farm. It had been hard enough for her to hold onto what remained of her life with no man and a child. She wasn't about to have her daughter relive the struggles and hardships of her own life. The best Mattie could tell, the baby couldn't be any bigger than a tadpole at this point. If she acted quickly, there was still time.

Chapter Eight
The Barter

Vancie was used to being worked over for church, but this Saturday and Sunday morning had been particularly trying. Mattie had boiled her in the tin tub like a batch of crawdads on Saturday, scraping over her skin with a hard-bristled brush and a cake of lye soap. By Sunday morning, a new dress had appeared from nowhere, and for the first time in her life her mother had pinched her cheeks until she thought they would bleed before applying a light coat of reddish powder to them. A small, silver cross had been hung around her neck, and she was hauled out the door, loaded like grain into the buckboard, and driven to church in Episcopalian silence. She and her mother had taken their pew in the old Green River Church for one of its last services before being vacated in the fall for the new church rising on the hill above the transforming town. Who knew that the arrival of one stranger in town could create such a ruckus?

Mr. Hill sat just two rows in front of them in his Sunday finest. Within days of his arrival in Tugaloo, he had bought the failing mercantile, and in rapid succession, other buildings downtown had taken on new ownership and new vitality. The small town buzzed with carpenters, masons, and painters as the community underwent a period of renewal and excitement unlike any other in its history. Mr. Hill's wealth had become legend, and his reputation in Tugaloo soared as small portions of his largesse trickled out to the hardscrabble folks scattered throughout the hills surrounding town. First the railroad, and now this. Of all of the changes, perhaps the most stunning was the new Green River Episcopal Church whose spire rose above the ridgeline of Tugaloo.

Vancie had grown used to the clenched jaw of her mother in recent days, but she was puzzled by her mother's detached presence in church. After a while, she made an imaginary line from her mother's steely stare to the object of its attention, and it seemed to lead to Mr. Hill. Her curiosity at the end of the service only rose as she watched her mother beat a hasty path to Mr. Hill and engage him in a very long, hushed conversation in the corner of the church. Halfway through their conversation, Vancie felt a cold chill as though being watched from her abandoned pew in the now-nearly-empty church. Turning her head to see when her mother might be ready to go, she met the methodical stare of Jagger Hill as he eyed her up and down. Vancie felt like a horse at auction having her teeth bared and hooves inspected. There was more whispering between her mother and Mr. Hill, but this time, it ended in formal smiles and polite handshakes.

Without a word, her mother retrieved her and escorted her to their buckboard. It would be nearly a week before her mother finally told her that she had been bartered away to Jagger Hill for the price of the remaining debt on the Keller Farm and the promise of a privileged life for her daughter as the first lady of Tugaloo. Days later, she was wrapped in white silk and a veil, delivered red-eyed to a private service at the unfinished church on the hill, married to Jagger Hill, and later that night raped by him for the first of countless times. Each time, she survived by holding tight to her memory of the tenderness of Josiah Buckland. Numbing herself to all other things, she retreated into the solitude and darkness of her own private hell, which she would not share with another living soul.

Vancie never blamed her mother. How could she have known? Though reluctant, in the end, Vancie knew that she had agreed to the marriage. Life with Jagger had hung before her, tinged with darkness perhaps, but solid, safe, and substantial. A life with Josiah at that time had appeared ethereal and uncertain, all heart and no head. How could anyone have ever known by outward appearances? Jagger Hill had not been watched long enough to see what kind of fruit fell from his tree. The Almighty in heaven might see the human heart, but the rest of His dumb beasts were subject to the mistakes of judgments made with the eyes.

Although Vancie wanted to die, she knew that she would live. She knew that she would live when she looked into the eyes of her sweet baby boy and saw, staring back at her, the blue of her own eyes and the gray flecks of Josiah Buckland's eyes. She knew she would live because Jagger had finally tired of her and sought his satisfaction from Delilah Hart and others in a bed above one of his many businesses in town. She was a mother now and would live at least, for the well-being of her child.

Chapter Nine
Delilah Hart

Delilah Hart lay sprawled out on her big mahogany bed, clothed in a pair of pink bloomers and nothing more. Her silk sheets had been pushed down to her footboard. Two girls in their early twenties sat on each side of her bed, alternately fanning themselves and then their madam with paper church fans. It was that unbearable time of afternoon in the summer when every breath of air stilled and the cicadas droned. Even though all of the doors in the hallway were flung open, there was no breeze to catch. A clock on the mantel ticked each sultry minute as her girls fished small chips of ice from a metal bowl and ran them across Delilah's glistening forehead. She allowed the resulting moisture to creep in small rivulets across her cheeks, down her neck, and around her ample breasts.

"Thank God for ice stored during long mountain winters and for the connections in town to have portions of it delivered on deadly summer afternoons."

Delilah Hart was out of uniform. Although her profession required few clothes in the late evening, what really made her feel naked was the complete absence of makeup.

The heat and humidity of the morning and afternoon had robbed her of every dab of rouge, powder, eye treatment, and perfume. Though still a good-looking woman in her natural state, she wouldn't be caught dead without the full application of every weapon in her arsenal, each of which was spread out on her dressing table across the room. It just wasn't professional, and she knew that she'd have to pull herself together during the next few hours. She was hoping and praying for rain. Most summer afternoons in the mountains, clouds would gather, the air would still and thicken, and the sky would weep cooling rain for an hour or more. On those days, it was a whole lot easier to rise from bed, apply her face, pull on layers of clothing, and sashay down the stairs to meet her gentlemen callers in her full glory. On the days it didn't rain, every bit of the same preparation had to be executed, but the process was carried out in abject misery. She lay still, waiting to hear which type of day this would be. Within moments, her answer came. The brilliant light outside of her windows dimmed, birds became silent, and the first distant rumbles of thunder reached her ears. Her breasts rose as she heaved a great sigh of relief. Soon, the cooling rain poured off of the eaves of the roof, past her window, and spattered into the dirt below.

With a wave of her hand and a slight smile of appreciation, she dismissed the girls, who exited with the chilled bowl and closed the door gently behind them. Delilah sat up in bed, her breasts filling and sagging only slightly as she swung her feet downward, fishing for her slippers. Finding them, she rose, retrieved her sheer dressing gown, and pulled it onto her bare shoulders. The room had not yet completely cooled, so she didn't bother to button the front as she proceeded to a small table without a mirror. She sat lightly, picked up a one-bristled brush, and began to dab the veins of leaves onto the small, white porcelain plate in front of her. Every working woman needed a pastime, and Delilah's was tole painting. Although usually the distraction of dried up spinsters in the South, Delilah found the silence and fine detail of the craft soothing. Several years ago, a botanist passing through the area had dropped in for the evening and, in gratitude, had left his sketchbook as part of his payments for services rendered to him. For a long time afterward, Delilah paged through the journal and marveled at the amazing variety and beauty of the flora. One day, she had gotten brave, purchased a few white plates, paint, and brushes from the mercantile and set to work. Her first attempts were crude, but her skill improved. Now, she found herself able to duplicate the art of the botanist. It felt good to take pride in her efforts. Today, a small display of trillium took shape before her. Suddenly becoming aware of time, she changed locations to the mirrored table on the other side of the room.

This was her work table. Dozens of cosmetics spread out before her. Expertly, she selected small jars and began the transformation for the work hours of the day. By the time social hour began at eight, she would be the fantasy of every farm boy, merchant, peddler, and lumberjack cued up for the evening to spend time with her and her girls. This being a weeknight, she had to look especially good because she would probably be spending most of her evening with Jagger Hill. Ever since he had settled in, he had become a frequent customer at Delilah Hart's house. At first, she had fixed him up with some of the younger women. However, word had come back to Delilah quickly that Jagger took his greatest satisfaction in inflicting pain. If he had been some two-bit farmer, she would have thrown him down the stairs herself. However, Jagger's wealth and growing power created a shield of immunity for his cruelty. Although there was no pleasure in the job, Delilah decided to take the bastard on herself rather than run the risk of him hurting one of her girls. Jagger fucked like a lineman driving railroad spikes, but Delilah knew her limits. She kept a small resolver in the drawer by her bed and knew how to use it if necessary.

Dabbing a last layer of powder across her cheeks and bosom, Delilah rose from her dressing table, cinched up her breasts, stepped into her gown, and pulled it up around her. She rarely felt remorse about her work. Her profession had begun early and had saved her from starvation. However, last week she had caught sight of Jagger's wife as her buggy rolled down the rutted main street of Tugaloo. There had been such sorrow in the young woman's face. She knew that most of that came from Jagger, but for the first time, she thought about the women of the men in her life. The thought had left her dead inside, so she quickly retreated back upstairs to her sanctuary. No time for such thoughts tonight. Her visitors awaited her.

Chapter Ten
The Ferryman

Josiah Buckland may have arrived in Tugaloo at noontime, but he had left in the dead of night. Mr. Coble had come to him after dinner with the news of Vancie's impending marriage to Jagger Hill. He thought of begging her to reconsider, but what incantation could he have spoken to undo the betrayal that had fallen upon her? Truth be known, his own anger and pride hadn't contributed to reconciliation. He hated to turn his back on all of the kindnesses that Mr. Coble had extended to him, but after the delivery of the news he said a tearful goodbye to Phineus Coble, threw his few worldly goods into a sack, tossed it over his shoulder, and eased out the back door of the livery.

Josiah quickly slipped out of town and made long strides for hours, putting as much distance between himself and the source of his pain as he possibly could. Although it violated all of his instincts, he was on the first of a series of roads and trails that would take him back to the high country. He had no idea what he would do when he got there: his parents were long gone. He had no siblings and his extended family had never immigrated from the highlands of Scotland. He was, once again, completely on his own. As morning neared, Josiah was stranded on the banks of the upper stretches of the Green River. He could go no further without the help of the ferryman. Searching the banks of the river for the scoundrel, he saw the old man's raft bobbing up and down in the early mists of the morning a few dozen feet from the riverbank. In order to provide a little extra protection from unexpected strangers and wild animals, the old man had anchored the craft a little way out in the channel.

At first, the raft appeared to be abandoned, but as Josiah peered into the obscurity of the near dawn, there was a stirring of the mist and a figure rose up slowly from the craft. Josiah found himself involuntarily stepping backward as the apparition came into sharper focus. Rising before him was the broad-shouldered figure of a silver-bearded man over six feet tall. The frightful thing about the old man was that he was armed not with pistol or rifle, but with some type of spear. He stood astride the ferry, still shrouded in semi-darkness, lower legs wreathed in mists. The ferryman was holding a small, crudely made, two-pronged triton tipped with a frog in his right hand.

"Why, hello, Boy. Come to join me for some grub?" the old haint shouted.

Josiah snapped back to his senses and realized that the ferryman had been on his knees, gigging the last of his breakfast under the late-night shroud before the sun chased his prey away. The ferryman used his muscled arms to draw the rope from the water and haul the craft back to the shoreline. Josiah got a better look at his breakfast host as the raft drew closer. The man's bespectacled, lined face emerged from the mists topped with a floppy, old broad-brimmed hat lying lightly atop his damp head. One corner of his chin was lined with tobacco stains and additional streaks trailed down into the tangle of his beard. His slightly stooped frame was draped in faded overalls. He had seen the man before.

"Ain't much of a talker, I see," said the old man as he lurched from the raft onto the bank of the river. "Catfish got your tongue?" he quipped, chuckling softly at his own wit as he whipped a straight-bladed knife from a creel at his waist.

Josiah once again instinctively took a step backward. "Why, no. Nothing has got my tongue," retorted Josiah. "I just need me a way across the river."

The old man hobbled to a small fire ring on the riverbank, struck a small piece of flint against the metal of his knife blade, and ignited the preset tinder piled up in the middle. A small blaze rose up, and the ferryman added twigs and then sticks in a methodical fashion. Once the blaze was secure, he dropped the creel next to a flat rock nearby, fished out the first of its contents, expertly sliced the heads from the squirming frogs, and cleaved off their back legs. Silently, he returned to the raft, retrieved a cast iron pan, tossed a bit of fatback into it, and dropped the frog legs into the soon sizzling skillet. The aroma of frog flesh, salt, and fat filled the morning air.

"Never, answered my question, Boy. Want some grub? And by the way, ain't I seen you before?" the old man grumbled as he stirred the contents of the pan.

"Well, yes, I would like something to eat, and you saw me a while back when I crossed the river the other direction when I was headed down from the hills."

Josiah remembered his first crossing painfully. Without any money, he had had to part with a silver belt buckle that had belonged to his father in order to settle his debt with the ferryman. He didn't suspect that the spirit of charity had fallen upon him since then, so he anticipated that there would once again be a painful price to get back to the other side. The ferryman leaned in a little closer, peering through the muddied lenses of his spectacles.

"Well, a lot of people pass this way, but I do seem to recollect seeing you 'afore," grunted his cook as he squirted tobacco juice to one side of the fire.

You ought to remember me, you old thief, thought Josiah. It wasn't that he denied anyone a living, but the belt buckle had been worth a considerable amount more than he would have paid if he had silver coin. Nothing had come back to him in the exchange. At least this time, he had a few coins, pressed into his hand by Mr. Coble as he left, and he was getting breakfast out of the deal to even up his last trip on the ferry.

When breakfast was golden brown, the old man set the pan on the ground between them and let Josiah gingerly retrieve his portion from the scalding grease. Though some town folk might have turned up their noses at the contents of the pan, meat of any kind was a rare treat for the boy. Josiah blew on each leg until it cooled, pulled the meat from the bones with his teeth, chewed with gusto, and sucked the bones until the last drop of grease was gone. Releasing a sigh of contentment, he balanced back on his haunches.

The ferryman broke the silence of the meal, announcing, "Now, that will be one quarter dollar for your passage and another quarter dollar for your grub."

Josiah launched to his full height and spat, "What! That is robbery. You never told me that you were charging me anything for my breakfast. I ought to go back to town and bring the sheriff down on you, you old reprobate!"

Menacingly, the ferryman replied, "Settle down there, sonny boy. I just asked you if you wanted any of my grub. You could have said *no*. Now, you don't have to cross this river, but you owe me for that food. By God, you will be paying me."

The crook reached over to the rock, retrieved his knife, and wiped frog guts and blood into the dew of the morning grass. Josiah was madder than hell after being jilted and now robbed, but he was no fool. Somehow, the old devil had calculated exactly how much money was in his pocket. It would cost him everything but his life to settle accounts with the ferryman and continue his journey. The last thread of his dignity was going to be left on this side of the river, but Josiah would just have to silently accept this butt kicking. His only comfort was that nothing would ever bring him back this way again. The boy fished into the deepest recesses of his pocket, extracted the two silver coins, and dropped them into the eagerly extended wrinkled hand. The ferryman smiled back in return, exposing the gaps left by several missing teeth.

Without further ado, the two of them kicked dirt onto the remaining embers of the breakfast fire, stepped lightly onto the ferry, pulled up the rope to draw them to the other side, and began Josiah's silent retreat from everything that he had found and loved during the past year. The ferryman looked down at the boy stoically. He had lost count years ago of how many country simpletons he'd shaken down. The problem for him now was that the thrill was gone, and all that remained was the mind-numbing drudgery of crossing and re-crossing the river.

Chapter Eleven
The Wood Carver

Like an executioner, Josiah Buckland
stood in the yard of his homestead, an ax
clinched tightly in both hands raised to its ze-
nith above him. Time and time again the
blade fell with violence, cleaving hunks of
the trunk of the chestnut tree. The wrath of
the noonday sun beat down upon his head and
bare torso. He lost himself in sorrow, pain,
fury, and sweat as the ax rose and fell in
rhythmic cadence. Although he had left her
behind in Tugaloo months before, the specter
of Vancie Keller occupied every waking moment and haunted the darkest recesses of his
nights. Josiah remained deeply wounded by
her rejection, but he had been driven to a state
of near madness by Phineus Coble's news of
her marriage to Jagger Hill. Every long-con-
sidered strategy of reconciliation had fallen
like flaming bridges across insurmountable
chasms. Faint hope in an instant became fatal
despair. He had lost her. Josiah Buckland,
young and foolish, had lost the light of his life
to the darkest and most corrupt soul that he'd
ever encountered.

He paused for a moment, sweat dripping from every part of his body, and shud-

dered in the noonday heat at the memory of his encounter with Jagger Hill on the sidewalk in Tugaloo. The hair on the nape of his neck rose in spite of the sweat as the vision of Hill congealed in his brain. Josiah then did the only thing that he had found to be effecttive in relieving the tyranny of his thoughts: he moved.

Hitching a chain to one end of the remaining six feet of the log, he dragged it across the dust, weeds, and chicken shit of his yard into the shed beside of the barn. He had thought about killing Jagger Hill, but Phineus Coble finally made him accept that Vancie Keller was bound to him by the iron manacles of the law. After several tortured nights, Josiah had finally gathered his few possessions and retreated to the only other home he'd ever known. It would never be where he wished to be, but he'd simply have to make the best of the choices, other than murder, that remained available to him.

Since his return to his father's old homestead in the high country, the shed had become his sanctuary from the pain of the outside world. Dark and musty from old hay, the outbuilding provided relief from the noonday sun, yet the cracks in the roof and sideboards still emitted enough light for his craft. Josiah had become a woodcarver. Farming had never been a profitable enterprise in the thin, rocky soil of the highlands. With the felling of many of the great trees from disease, Josiah had been gifted the raw material to churn out a steady stream of chairs, sideboards, bed frames, and wagon wheels. His new profession lent itself well to the daily, practical needs of the thrifty, no-nonsense Scotsmen who populated the mountaintops of the Blue Ridge. As he heaved the roughed-out log upright in his workspace, he knew that it would never support the weary bodies of his neighbors at night, house their tableware, or rock their children.

Josiah knew that a lovely, young woman lay imprisoned within this wood. She had called to him in his dreams now for weeks, begging to be set free from captivity. Now, like a knight of old, Josiah had come to her rescue. He picked up a small hatchet from his work table and proceeded to hack away at the bark of the chestnut. With each blow, he exposed part of her smooth skin beneath the coarse shell of her imprisonment. For hours upon hours, day after day, Josiah hacked, gouged, sawed, chipped, and polished until the beauty of her face emerged, the tresses of her hair cascaded over smooth shoulders, and the elegant arms of her body wrapped themselves in front of her around a great mystery. Driven beyond reason, Josiah left a great bulge on the front of the emerging figure where it should not have been. Days ago, the bulk of her breasts, hips, back and limbs had been winnowed down to their scale in the real world. However, without reason, a great mass had remained in her midsection. Josiah stepped back in wonder as he puzzled over the crude, formless mass that marred the midsection of the emerging essence of Vancie Keller. He couldn't understand why his vision of the beautiful figure blurred in her midsection. Perhaps fatigue had gotten the best of him at the end of a long workday. In exasperation and defeat, he slowly placed his tools on his workbench and retreated from the shed for his evening meal.

Chapter Twelve
Mama Lois

Mama Lois sat bolt upright in her cast iron bed at the end of a dark hallway in her old farmhouse. The golden strands of her hair had turned to the bluish-gray of gunmetal and were now wrapped tightly about her head like a diadem. Her grandson, James, had occasionally seen her tresses unfurled when Mama Lois pulled loose all of the pins and clips that held it in place and unleashed it to its full length down to her knees. She would sit in a small rocker on the back porch taking sections of it in her silver comb and work rainwater from the barrel down the strands until she eventually squeezed it from the tips into a basin at her feet.

In those days, when her tongue remained sharp and her temper quick, the boy thought of the stories that he had been told of Medusa and her strands of snakes. When James was young, the old woman seemed to hate the boy, more for simply breathing than anything he'd actually done wrong. But in recent years as her mind dimmed, her heart softened and her face brightened any time he entered the room. It brightened more than when Mattie brought her meals, more even than when her own daughter, Vancie, appeared.

James found her affection even more mysterious than her hatred had been. Whatever grudge had existed on the part of the old woman had burned away like the sultry dampness of an August morning after a night of rain. Mama Lois had simply lived long enough to forget precisely who and what it was that she was supposed to hate. She was lucky that James was a boy and not a man. A puppy could be whipped and still come back time and again believing that a stroke rather than a swat was just around the corner. A dog would strike back.

"Hey, Mama Lois!" James chattered as he emerged from the darkness of the hallway into the full morning light of the old woman's bedroom.

He leapt up on the bed, rattling her breakfast tray as he snuggled in beside her.

"Well, good morning to you, you rascal." the old woman squealed as she pushed her tray down to the foot of the bed.

A rooster crowed down in the yard beneath her window.

"Now boy, what is it that the rooster says?"

"Why, Mama Lois, the rooster says, 'Doctor Gaston! Doctor Gaston'!" responded the boy with pride.

Mama Lois cackled with laughter and hugged the boy close to her. This was their great secret. James had discovered that Mama Lois could talk to all of the barnyard animals and understand their every reply. She had explained that the rooster was a particularly good friend of hers. Any time he saw that old sawbones, Dr. Gaston, heading up the road in his buggy, the bird would scream out the doctor's name to give Mama Lois time to lock the parlor door and buy herself a day or two of reprieve from his endless probing, sticking, and fussing.

Their days were spent in endless hours of barnyard tales, gliding on the front porch swing, and singing silly songs that Mama Lois had been taught as a child in Ireland. Mattie did all of the cooking now, and Big John kept up the garden. Mama Lois was free all day long to lighten James's heart and cure him of the endless melancholy of life with his mother and father back at Orchard Cove. Wednesdays at Mama Lois's were days to breathe deeply and freely, to be silly, loud and juvenile, all things that were banned at his father's house.

"Sing that song to me again, Mama Lois, the one about the dog, the cat, and the fiddle."

She did, and James, bouncing, leapt over the old woman's legs each time that the cow jumped over the moon.

"Tell me that you will never leave me, Mama Lois. Tell me that you will always love me."

The old woman pulled him tightly to her side and replied, "He will never leave nor forsake thee."

James was comforted by her tone and most of her words. He puzzled over her use of "He" for a while, but finally wrote it off to the dimming of her mind. She made many small mistakes these days.

"He will never leave nor forsake thee," the old woman chanted once again before lapsing into her morning nap.

Chapter Thirteen
Of Pear Trees and Plott Hounds

Many people thought James to be an unusual looking child. He had clearly inherited the golden hair of his mother and her prominent cheek bones, but the combination of his mother's features and his odd bluish-gray eyes set him apart from all of the other boys at his school. The fact that his father owned more than half of Tugaloo didn't help either. His father had pumped a fortune into the town, but that hadn't gone far to tamp down its citizens' jealousies. Though strong, James often found himself an outsider and suffered when he heard the whispered taunts of "ghost boy" or "wolf child." The rejection of his peers drove him to entertain himself on his own, so when he could escape the watchful eye of his father, James wandered the forests and creeks of Jagger Hill's considerable land holdings, following streams, turning over rocks, and tracking game.

Once in the woods, James felt safe from his peers and his father. Though his father had hundreds of acres of land, his only joy in nature seemed to come from owning a large piece of it. James was often deeply disturbed by his father's orientation to the earth. Last spring, the normally bountiful pear tree on the front lawn at Orchard Cove blossomed, but by fall it had borne no fruit. James bounded down the steps of the manor house one beautiful fall morning and froze in his tracks. Jagger Hill stood like a lumber jack in the front yard of his newly-occupied barony with the sleeves of his dress shirt rolled up, ax in hand. The white steps and yellow-sided levels of the mansion soared before Jagger like an ostentatious wedding cake. With horror, James realized that the object of Jagger's wrath was about to be his favorite tree.

"But, Father, pear trees don't bear fruit every fall. Sometimes, they just store up for a big harvest the next year!" pleaded James.

If Jagger Hill heard the boy, he paid no mind. The ax rose and fell, slicing into the tree trunk and into the boy's heart. The boughs of the tree and their golden leaves quivered with each blow, and before he knew what he was doing, James had crossed the yard and wrapped his eight-year-old arms around Jagger's legs.

"Please, Father, just give it another…"

Before he could even finish his sentence, James felt the right side of his head explode as the back side of Jagger Hill's hand struck him with stunning force. James rolled across the lawn, felt the light of day darken, and was momentarily deafened by the ringing in his ears. When his hearing returned, he heard his father spewing invectives:

"No goddamned tree is going to suck nutrients and water from my land and give nothing back in return. Not for the long haul of even the short one. 'The tree that does not bear fruit is cut down and cast into the fire.'"

It was the first and only time that James ever heard his father utter a word of scripture. The blows to the root of the tree resumed as James lay stunned on the ground until he heard the crack of the trunk as the ancient tree toppled backward and shook the ground. By late in the day, the tree had been sawed to kindling with crosscut saws by the help. Old lumber from the barn, dead brush, and lamp oil were added to the wreckage, and by dark, the prophetic words of Jagger Hill rang true as the sweet smell of burning pear wood rose into the starry night sky.

As devastated as James was by the destruction of his favorite tree, he had no notion of what other brutal lessons would be driven home by his father in the coming year. By the next summer, the pear tree had been largely forgotten except upon the rare occasion that James stumbled upon the remaining indentation in the lawn when he played there. Last fall had brought an unusual act of kindness shortly after the destruction of the tree. Jagger Hill had purchased a handsome, tall hound and a matching bitch from the estate of a timber baron on the other side of Sassafras Mountain. The baron had been experimenting with a new type of hound that would be fearless in ferreting out the last of the black bears that ruled the high country. Mr. Plott had nearly mastered the new breed, and upon hearing of a hound more fearless than a bear, Jagger was consumed with lust to own one of the first breeding pairs. Late in the spring, the male had his way when the bitch came into heat, and by fall, eight puppies whimpered in the run by the barn.

James was overwhelmed with joy as he passed the pen with the writhing puppies each day. He could smell the aroma of new puppy as he passed the enclosure, but knew better than to think that he'd ever touch them. Jagger Hill had owned dogs in the past, and he owned them as he owned everything in his dominion, exclusively. At one point, two of Jagger's dogs had dropped their litters the same week. A few months later, thirteen pups yapped behind the fence, well beyond the reach of James's eager little hands. This time, his father shocked him by announcing that James was to pick and name one of the young male hounds. Jagger hoped that ownership of such a masculine beast might make a real boy out of his doe-eyed son. The boy spent too much time with his weak-willed mother, and, if there was ever to be anything hanging between the boy's legs, it was going to require intervention on Jagger's part. Upon hearing his father's offer of a pup, James couldn't control his delight and danced around his father like a pup himself, proclaiming, "His name is Sport. His name is Sport. That's my pup's name!"

Jagger looked down with mild disdain, and left the boy to his embarrassing exuberance.

In the coming months, James and Sport were as inseparable as Jagger would allow, but James had been given strict instructions by his father "not to ruin the animal." This meant, at least in Jagger's presence, that he was to show the dog no signs of physical affection. James was to follow a strict regimen of controlled feeding, teaching voice commands, and the gradual introduction of game scents to awaken its primal instincts. When rabbits and other game were killed by the help for the family table, James was allowed to take the pelts to expose the pup to their hides and the scent of blood.

James would have done anything to have a dog of his own, so he followed Jagger's instructions with great precision. However, when he knew that his father was safely away in town, James would occasionally steal a hug from his new best friend. After much preparation that summer, the day came for Sport to get his first official hunting trial with James and Jagger Hill. By then, Sport could track the carcass of a rabbit that James had dragged through the grounds of Orchard Cove and hidden in the brush for a reward when found. Today, the pup would have his first go at live rabbits.

Jagger descended the steps of the house with his gun over his shoulder. Within an hour, Sport had jumped a rabbit in the brush along an old fence line, and the hunt was on. James thrilled as Sport made his first shrill attempts at baying as he pursued the rabbit. Instinct and older dogs would teach the pup to slowly circle the rabbit back to where it had been jumped. Jagger ran back for interception, rapidly outpacing James's shorter legs. James struggled behind, wading through the swampy areas of the lower pasture and painfully fighting his way through patches of excruciating cane briars. Still a considerable distance behind, James's heart pounded out of his chest with pride when he heard the echoing report of Jagger's gun.

Tearing his pants as he ripped his way loose from the briars, James crested the hill and gazed down the slope with horror. Jagger stood at the bottom of the hill with a slight wisp of smoke rising from his gun. Sport lay at the foot of a large oak tree in a pool of his own blood. Running up to his father, James opened his mouth to scream, but no sound came. His father broke down his gun, ejecting the shells.

"Damn fool dog chased a squirrel up a tree rather than follow the trail of the rabbit. You can never fix that in a dog."

Chapter Fourteen
Big John

Big John stood deep in the growing darkness of a pit of his own making. The last thing Miss Lois had told him that she needed was a new root cellar. Now, she lay dying in the house in the last hours of her life. The old cellar had been slowly crumbling for years, so Big John spent the last few days digging in the earth to keep himself out from underfoot as womenfolk tended to her needs. As he worked, he could occasionally hear the keening of Miss Vancie as the hour neared.

Yesterday, as he cut the walls of the cellar with his spade, he could hear his daddy's voice, "Now, John, you make all of them walls in that ditch straight. Don't you go messing up. One of these here days, somebody will dig up this here ditch and say, 'That man that dug this ditch, he dug it up for the Lord. It sure is purty.'"

It had been a long time since he'd heard his daddy's voice in his head. He tried not to think of such things. His daddy had died young in years, but old in body and mind. He was worked to death on a cotton plantation near the coast. Big John tried to remember as little from those days as possible. He hated taking his clothes off at night and seeing what he could of the ridges that marked his back, torso, and chest. A whip had engraved them when he was a boy. There would have been more of them, but as soon as the war ended, he had taken off with Aunt Mattie for the hills. His mama and daddy were both dead by then. He and Aunt Mattie ran for the mountains because they were the farthest thing they knew from the coast. There weren't many black people in the mountains. Many of the white people blamed them for the war, but the Kellers had taken him and Aunt Mattie in. They probably had worked about as hard on the Keller farm as they had on the plantation, but the Kellers worked shoulder-to-shoulder with them. Mr. Marcus had done his best, but he was busted up bad from the war. Miss Lois had a sharp tongue, but she worked from sunup to sundown as long as Big John had known her.

Big John didn't care. He was free. Though he didn't own the earth he dug in, he wasn't owned by the man and woman who did. He loved the earth, its smell in the spring, and its touch as he busted coal black clots of it in his enormous hands. Unlike most men, he didn't shy away from plowing fields, digging ditches, planting trees, or burying the dead. The winter earth was hard as he cut out the new cellar walls, and Big John knew that he'd be digging in the frozen earth again within days, this time, no deeper than six feet. It would be his last favor to the old woman for taking him and Aunt Mattie in. He tried not to think what would become of the two of them when Miss Lois passed. Miss Vancie was a good woman too, but she had gone and married the devil. He'd seen that man's kind many times before when he was a boy. Every time Mr. Jagger's shadow fell on him, Big John made a cross in the yard from sticks to undo the hex. Just thinking about him gave Big John the chilly bumps, so picking up his spade, he cut a little deeper into the cold dark earth and found a rhythm of work that drove all thoughts from his head.

Chapter Fifteen
The Ice Storm

Sleet pelted the brim of James's hat like pellets of steel. If Big John hadn't dug Mama Lois's grave yesterday, the funeral would have been postponed. A front had blown into the mountains during the night, bringing with it an icy mist and an imminent threat of snow. Snow might indeed come, but for now, icy projectiles continued to fall in sheets as the small band of humans huddled like cattle beneath the fir tree at the back of Mama Lois's house.

James watched his own breath materialize and then dissipate inches from his face. In spite of his heavy coat and broad-brimmed hat, the cold sneaked into the seams where one piece of his wool clothing met another. The boy pressed himself close to his mother and felt the warmth of her gloved hand as he reached up and took her small, strong hand into his own. Her grip reminded him of Mama Lois. Even in the last days of her life, as cancer ate away at her insides, her grip retained the tensile strength of a fencing foil. James used to wince and attempt to pull his hand away when Mama Lois would take it in her own. He could never reconcile her small frame, especially in old age, to the crushing power of her grip. Perhaps it came from year upon year of picking cotton in the flatlands during her own childhood and youth. Perhaps it just came to those who had lived long, worked hard, and suffered unbearable sorrows. There were things of the earth that could break the body, mind, and spirit of the half-hearted. In order to remain in the shadowlands of this world, the strong-willed had to clutch tightly to life, lest they be snatched away without warning. James tightened his grip on his mother's hand as the preacher droned on.

Mama Lois had been what the people of the hills referred to as a hard-shelled Baptist. No card playing, no drinking, no dancing, and no musical instruments even in church. On a few occasions, James had attended church with Mama Lois late in her ninety years of life. Though a religious woman in a severe sort of a way, Mama Lois said that her absences from church in her later years would be forgiven because an old woman has lost all of the padding on her rump to be able to sit respectfully and endure hours of hellfire and damnation preaching.

"The Maker understands such things and makes concessions to the bony-assed late in life."

When she was in church, she sat straight-backed, her shawl wrapped tightly around her shoulders and her iron gray spectacles pressed tightly to her face. Mama Lois was a stern woman, but James had seen her on the periphery of a barn dance with a smile stealing across her lips and her foot lightly tapping the ground. Even a lifetime of hardships and eons of church-going in the mountains could not completely extinguish the flame lighted in her family in more pagan corners of Ireland.

To keep damp that flame, Mama Lois never missed the foot washing services on Sunday nights. If there was indeed any sacrament in life to counter the fires of Hell, it was foot washing. There was a rawness in peeling off socks and stockings, baring calloused, smelly feet, and walking forward barefooted and rooted to the ground. The ritual stripped away all pretense of being anything more than the dust of the Earth.

"Ashes to ashes and dust to dust," droned the preacher as he scooped a handful of frozen black clods of earth and scattered it over the exposed pine box six feet below.

The boy felt a brutal sense of loss. His greatest loss was his grandmother, but Mama Lois's house had also been his sanctuary from his father and his tyrannical oppression at Orchard Cove. Now there was nowhere to hide. James lifted his grayish-blue eyes from the hole, tears streaming across his frozen face, and looked up at the faces of his mother, Mattie, and Big John. Tears streamed down all of their faces too, and James imagined them simply becoming salt-tinged additions to the sleet as it continued its assault upon all things warm and living.

The only dry eyes he saw were the dark orbs of Jagger Hill as he stared out blankly across the mist-shrouded ridges. Though his mother's husband and his own father, Jagger stood apart from all of the other mourners, touching and being touched by no one. His feet shuffled impatiently in the frozen slush beneath them, and James sensed his father's readiness to bolt for the carriage upon the utterance of the last "Amen." Without warning, James realized that Jagger Hill had shifted his gaze and was now suddenly staring back at him with a venomous countenance and furrowed brow. Jagger Hill, in the lead-like grayness of the day, had been caught off guard once again by his son's haunting, transcendent gaze.

Where in hell did he get those eyes? His bitch of a mother has blue eyes, and my own are nearly black. Why does that boy look like a goddamned wolf staring back at me? And where have I seen those eyes before?

Jagger racked his brain searching back through the years.

James faintly smiled at his father, but his smile was not returned.

Chapter Sixteen
Encounter

It had been a hard year for James. The death of his dog and the devastating loss of Mama Lois had left the boy hollow inside. Finally, a morning dawned without his father in the house or the prospect of his return for the entire day. Jagger had gone to Asheville on business and would not return until late that night. James had been banned from the house to "give his mother time to rest."

After wandering aimlessly about the yard for a while, James wildly ran several miles down the road from Orchard Cove and plunged into the forest. Escaping the heat of the day and the oppression of home, the cool of the forest enveloped James and slowly stilled his racing heart. For over an hour, the boy moved from tree to tree in the pathless woods, dodging the occasional laurel thicket and briar patch. After great effort, he came to what appeared to be a faint and crude trail. James wasn't even sure that it was a trail, but by mid-morning, the path took on greater definition, leading him deeper into the heart of the great forest.

By noon, his efforts had brought him to a small rippling stream, cascading noisily over rocks. He amused himself by turning over stones, looking for salamanders and crayfish beneath them, but the attractions of the stream paled in comparison to the allure of the thunderous noise coming from more deeply in the woods. James found the roar irresistible as he forced himself through the thickets lining the creek, edging nearer and nearer to the source of the fury. Within minutes, he emerged from the dark thickets of the forest into a small opening at the foot of a magnificent waterfall. The white foam of the cataract bounded from boulder to boulder as it leapt from the heights, descended the wall of the gorge, and plummeted into the boiling cauldron at its base. The cool mist billowing from the cauldron soothed his fatigue.

As clouds thinned overhead, the curtain of the fall morphed from gray to dazzling white. James's knees slowly buckled and his body fell to the rock beneath him. Kneeling, he was enveloped in light, mist, and sound as leaves rustled gently around him. James lost any sense or capacity for words. Everything became feeling. Later, when some ability to think and speak returned, the word that would finally come to him was "oneness." At Orchard Cove, everything was separate. There was house, mother, father, help, animals, and tree. Here, everything blurred. Here, everything was one and alive: sky, water, light, rock, and tree. The words separating these things seemed ridiculous. All things were one, and life pulsed in everything, even those things like rocks that James had always believed to be dead. Nothing was more or less alive than another. Nothing was more or less alive than himself. He heard his own heart beat in rhythm with wind, water, and trees. At first, everything just seemed to pulse with energy and life, but soon, James had the odd sensation of another joining him.

His eyes told him that he was alone in the forest, but his heart was at war with his eyes. There was Other, and it wasn't the birds in the trees or the trout in the stream. They were on his side. Whatever had joined James at the falls had joined them too. The sensation was so foreign that he had no words for it. Later, he would realize that this feeling might be what others called peace. James had known no peace in his life, but he knew the comfort of a quilt at night in the winter. Whatever came to him came in that way. It settled over and around him, but in the end, it was not *something* settling over him but rather *someone*.

In his bliss, James knew three things: if this presence continued to grow he would die from joy, this experience couldn't last, and finally, that he would spend the rest of his life seeking this sensation again. Too soon, he felt it slipping away. He wanted to cry out in despair and longing, but he knew that it would do no good. Whatever had come to him did not answer to him. Within moments, things were separate again. James was ravenously hungry, strangely sad, and frightened as he became aware of lengthening shadows. Rising from the rock, James turned away from the waterfall and marched silently toward his house. Fortunately, he found a more clearly marked trail for his return, and his trip home was uneventful. At one point, he saw what appeared to be an old, dilapidated building in the distance, but the sun was too low in the sky for any more exploring today.

Chapter Seventeen
The Church

The carriage slowly crested the ridge as it struggled for traction on the newly-graded road. Jagger's heart swelled with immeasurable pride as the white spire of the newest of his creations soared into the cobalt sky before him. This was a structure worthy of praise and a fitting focal point for gleaming Main Street. Every town worth its salt possessed a church that dwarfed all other structures and reminded everyone, every day, of what it was to come before magnificence. All of the dots scurrying back and forth in New Town, perhaps soon to be called Hillsdale, needed to be kept in perpetual remembrance of what it was to be small and insignificant.

For a few moments, he was lost in his own joys and had forgotten his travel companion, who was tucked into the far corner of the seat beside him. Vancie sat in silence, staring blankly ahead with her empty, azure eyes. The boy had been dropped off with Mattie at the Keller farm for her to mind a fever that sprung up in him the day before. Mattie and her nigger nephew kept up the place until Jagger could make arrangements to sell it. Whatever this day meant to Jagger, to Vancie it was just another day in an endless struggle to keep her withering soul alive. She walked in lands of shadow, oblivious to the town below, the gleaming white church before her, and the finery that enveloped her. Jagger had spared no expense for this day. The most luxuriant fabric in Charleston had been shaped to her hourglass figure. It tightened around her tiny waist and lifted her fully mature breasts to the observation, desire, and envy of every man and woman in the crowded sanctuary. They would all be sanctified in the best of their own clothes, but however polished on the outside, the coarseness of their insides would still harbor lust for her husband's wealth and the riches that nature had bestowed upon Vancie Hill.

According to the Gospel of St. John, no one had to tell Jesus what dwelled in the hearts of humans, and no one had to tell Vancie either. Her private musings were suddenly violated by the sharp crack of the buggy whip against the straining, damp flanks of their horses and the sharper crack of Jagger's tongue as he broke what remained of the quiet of a sad, Sabbath morning.

"Sit up straight, damn you! And slap a smile onto your stupefied face. I didn't spend a goddamned fortune in Charleston on clothes, hats, and jewelry to have you behave like some cowering yard dog this morning.

You are Mrs. Jagger Hill. Sit your ass up straight and act like it. We are about to pull up to the front of the church."

The carriage rested in a circular drive before the doors of the gleaming edifice. Throngs of people from the town below crowded the drive and entrance foyer of the church. Heads turned and eyes widened as the occupants dismounted.

"Why, Mr. and Mrs. Hill. Good morning to you. It's a fine building indeed, Sir. Yet another major step forward for our small town. Why, you're looking magnificent this morning, Mrs. Hill. Never prettier I would say," said someone in the crowd. Suddenly the chatter of the crowd was muted as the rector strode out onto the steps of the church and proclaimed to all of the faithful:

> Lift up your heads, O ye gates; and be ye lift up, ye everlasting doors; and the King of glory shall come in.
> 8 Who is the King of glory? It is the Lord strong and mighty, even the Lord mighty in battle.
> 9 Lift up your heads, O ye gates, and be ye lift up, ye everlasting doors; and the King of glory shall come in.
> 10 Who is the King of glory? Even the Lord of hosts, he is the King of glory. [Glory be to the Father, and to the Son: and to the Holy Ghost;

> As it was in the beginning, is now, and ever shall be: world without end. Amen.]

*****

Adoring townsfolk from all sides reached out to touch the Hills as they mounted the steps to the foyer. The hush of the elect already inside brought the new arrivals to silence within the coolness of the brilliant sanctuary. Light streamed in profusion through a miasma of colored glass as the sun broke through the morning mists of the mountains. Sonorous tones poured forth from the organ, which had been purchased on a whim while Jagger was in New York last spring.

After everyone took their seats, the liturgy of the Book of Common Prayer, 1662 began, and the first congregants of Green River Holy Episcopal Church spouted their prayers, praises, and petitions of consecration of a new church and a new day. Nothing of the newness of her surroundings penetrated Vancie's mind or heart. There was no new day, only another day and then another. She was jolted to awareness when it was time for her to move. Congregants dropped, mounted, and raised kneeling benches in preparation for the Eucharist. The priest raised a gleaming silver plate, pitcher, and chalice before her as Jagger subtly tightened his grasp on her elbow and bent her body to his will. The liturgist intoned the epistle:

2 Corinthians 6:14-17

'Be ye not unequally yoked together with unbelievers: for what fellowship hath righteousness with unrighteousness? And what communion hath light with darkness? And what concord hath Christ with Belial? Or what part hath he that believeth with an infidel?

'And what agreement hath the temple of God with idols? For ye are the temple of the living God; as God hath said, I will dwell in them, and walk in them; and I will be their God, and they shall be my people.'

She advanced down the aisle before him like a puppet on a string until she found herself before the newly-hired parish priest. Vancie numbly received the bread from his pale appendage in her cupped hands, dipped the morsel into the cup, and lifted it mechanically to her mouth. She felt a small part of her brain come to life, though it wasn't due to the overwhelming presence of the Magnum Mysterium. It was the faint aroma of the bread that revived Vancie with long-forgotten memories of the simple goodness of the kitchen, of flour, lard, and milk kneaded into the sustenance of life itself. Memories of her mother, her old wooden breadboard, and the burst of heat from her stove assaulted her mind, heart, and spirit. Vancie set her jaw and stifled simultaneous desires to cry and collapse beneath the weakening frame of her body.

At just the right moment, the sting of tannic wine burst forth from the morsel in her mouth and cleared her senses like smelling salts. She knew little of God and far less of church, but she returned to her pew, awake as she had not been in a long time. Sight, sound, and smell poured into the vacuum of her soul and nearly swept her away with its force. Color from the windows, robes, and worship implements dazzled her. Music permeated her very being, and the smells of candles and flowers soothed her. The benediction interrupted Vancie's rejuvenation.

"The peace of God, which passeth all understanding, keep your hearts and minds in the knowledge and love of God, and of his Son Jesus Christ our Lord: And the Blessing of God Almighty, the Father, the Son, and the Holy Ghost, be amongst you, and remain with you always. Amen."

Vancie turned to Jagger to see him discreetly spit the small purple-stained mass into his white handkerchief and effortlessly return it to his breast pocket.

Chapter Eighteen
Rosemary O'Shay

In the weeks following her last communion, Vancie's spirit remained strong, but terror crept into her heart as she watched her body slowly waste away. It began with dark circles under her eyes that refused to fade regardless of rest. She felt her body slowing incrementally each day as her waistline shrank, her hair thinned, and her gums bled. Before long, Vancie found herself bedridden from exhaustion. Although Jagger shunned her in disgust, he allowed Rosemary, one of the kitchen staff, to bring her meals and make weekly trips to the apothemcary and retrieve the medicines prescribed by Dr. Gaston. The ancient healer faithfully arrived at her bedside each week, mumbled a new diagnosis, and assured her of a better response to the next elixir.

She was no fool and paid him no mind. Vancie Keller knew dying when she saw it. She had recently seen it in the face of her own mother. Her fear was not for herself. Dying was her only escape route from Jagger Hill. Her terror was for James. With Momma Lois gone, James would be left with Jagger and no buffer between the boy and the man who believed himself to be his father. Even when assuming James his son, Jagger was unspeakably cruel to him. What would become of James without her between them? Jagger would never allow James to flee to Mattie, and her age made that an impossibility anyway. Mattie would invoke enough of Jagger's wrath when he discovered that Vancie had willed her parents' farm to her and Big John.

Somehow, she had to get James back to his own father, but Vancie had no idea where Josiah fled when he left town. Even if she knew where to find him, she was too weak to reach Josiah. Vancie knew that she would have to have an ally, but Jagger had so controlled her life since their marriage that her circle of friends was nonexistent. The only person she saw on a regular basis was Rosemary. Jagger had returned from a business trip to Boston with Rosemary O'Shay in tow. The poor girl had barely arrived from Ireland in full flight from famine when Jagger scooped her up to add to his unnecessarily large house staff. Jagger Hill collected human beings the way many people collected livestock or furniture.

He was particularly attracted to Rosemary because of her mastery of all things baked. Even in his bed at the hotel, he had been overcome by the aroma of bread, scones, pastries and pies rising up the stairway from the kitchen below. Before hard times descended upon her in the old country, she had immersed herself in the mysteries of wheat, rye, and barley. When the blight arrived, Rosemary risked her life by crossing an ocean in search of prosperity. Sharing secrets with poor Rosemary would be foolhardy and a risk that could cost her and James their lives, but she was going to have to trust somebody, and her options were limited.

Early the next day, Vancie reached out and pulled James to her bedside when he entered to give her a morning kiss.

"James, my darling, Momma has a gift this morning for you, but it's our secret and you must never share this gift with anyone other than one person."

Vancie pressed the golden watch into the boy's small palm. James's eyes widened as he fingered the timepiece.

"In the near future, a special friend of Mommy's is going to come to you. He will be tall, with brown hair and gray eyes. When you are introduced to this man, show him your special watch. Tell him that you know about the secret place in the back of the watch. You can trust this man. He is our friend. Show no one the watch other than him. Do as he says, and go with him if he asks."

James was puzzled but could tell from his mother's distressed look that now was not the time for questions. Sadness, illness and pain were etched in dark lines on his mother's face. Vancie's once glistening eyes had grown dull and distant. He allowed her head to fall back on the pillow and waited until her breathing became deeper and regular before he slipped silently from the room.

Later that morning, Rosemary brought Vancie's breakfast tray and methodically dropped her medicine into her tea. Rosemary's eyes widened to saucers as Vancie poured out her tale to the poor house servant.

"Your story is safe with me, Mistress Hill. Don't be to worrying. Just drink up your tea now and get yourself some rest. I will find him. I will find him for you."

Vancie fell back into a stupor and slept the remainder of the morning. Rosemary took her tray back to the kitchen, put her dishes in the sink, pulled a stool to the cabinet and put the dropper bottle in the far back corner of a high shelf above all of the medicines prescribed by Dr. Gaston. The dropper bottle now contained only spring water.

I am not a bad woman. Rosemary mused. *I would do the mistress no harm, but the mistress is weak like the stars, not strong like the sun and the moon.*

Her beauty had drawn Master Hill to her, but she knew that Jagger Hill was no admirer of beauty. Beauty was a fleeting fancy. Master Hill loved strength, and Rosemary knew that she was a strong woman. She had drawn her strength from the rocky earth that nursed the once-plentiful grains of Ireland. She alone in this house was a child of earth and worthy of a man like Jagger Hill. She alone was worthy of the life he could offer.

Chapter Nineteen
The Body

Vancie's body lay still, dwarfed by the sturdy walls of the chestnut box and silver ornamentation which now encased her. She was finally contained and subject to Jagger Hill's every whim.

"Now, now, pretty one, rest your weary body and mind. I'll take care of everything from now on." whispered Jagger.

He lied. He'd certainly take care of everything, but she was no longer that pretty. The high, fine cheekbones of her face, her ample bosom, and the redness of her lips remained thanks to the skill of the undertaker. Even so, he missed the grace of her movement as she swept about the house performing his will and the soft subservience of her hushed voice in response to his commands. What he didn't miss were her eyes. Well, the usual cowed look of them, perhaps. But not the white-hot flash that on the rarest of occasions revealed the rage and contempt she bore for him. As a final farewell to that spark of freedom which had remained in her eyes, Jagger reached into his vest pockets, removed two heavy gold coins, and pressed them firmly into her sockets. Stepping back, he found her beautiful once again.

Tomorrow, the stream of the bereaved would arrive. On Wednesday, the funeral would take place at his church with a late afternoon burial in the churchyard.

"In final victory, I will turn a skeleton key in the lock of the new Hill family crypt, grieve for the appointed number of days, and then set about the business of installing a new mistress of Orchard Cove," Jagger droned methodically.

His premature celebration was interrupted by a flash of orange in the darkness outside of the drawing room window. Jagger strode to the massive door of the house, threw it back against the wall, drew his pistol, and stepped onto the broad porch. In his wildest imaginings, he could not have anticipated what peered up from the center of the drive beneath him. That damned old black housekeeper from the Keller place stood trespassing in the darkness, flanked by other torch-bearing darkies four or five deep on either side. He had no reason to recognize any of her other shiftless conspirators, but the one immediately to her right might have been that old nigger preacher, Andy, from that ramshackle church in the woods.

"What do you want, washer woman, and what in the hell are you doing trespassing on my goddamned property in the middle of the night?"

For a moment, he was answered by the darkness of the evening. Mattie Fort stood before him, arms akimbo, eyes closed, and softly humming as she shifted her weight methodically from one foot to another. Without warning, she froze in place, her yellow eyes blazed to life, and a piercing cry escaped her lips that made the hair on the back of Jagger's neck spring up in response.

Pointing her crooked finger up from the small circle of light to the darkness above, Mattie keened, "Devil Man, you old Devil Man, the land I stand on; it ain't your land. The land which I stand on be the Earth. The Earth, it done been here before you, before me, even before the mountains and the hills were here. And the Lord of the Earth and of the heaven, He done sent me to you tonight. It don't be the ground that be damned by Him. You be damned by Him, and He done sent me to this house tonight to take that girl lying in there back to her mama in the ground, back to the earth of her farm, and back to other folk that you don't know nothing about. Get out of our way, Devil Man, and leave us to our work."

The absurdity of her challenge evoked an immediate and overwhelming impulse for Jagger to break into gales of laughter. But as his chest swelled and muscles tightened, an image paralyzed him mid-respiration. The piercing, yellow menace of the old woman's eyes as she drew a few steps closer to the bottom of the stairs, filled Jagger with dread.

She transformed before him into some primordial emblem of authority, power, and danger. The form of the washer woman faded and was replaced by a shapeless specter of the forest that stalked and disemboweled its prey in a silent frenzy of tooth and claw. For the first time in his life, Jagger Hill's confidence in himself cracked. Without warning, a deep hesitation seeped into that crack as the old woman's companions hummed and chanted some dark, sonorous incantations as they advanced toward the steps of his home. The reality that he didn't just face some old black bitch, but rather a phalanx of flaming might, congealed in his consciousness.

His hand slipped slowly to the trigger of his gun, which still hung tightly in his hand, but his merchant mind quickly calculated the bullets in the chamber and the foes before him. Even if he took some of them down, one torch was enough to reduce himself and all that he had labored for, to smoldering ruins. What if, in a reckless frenzy, they decided to use Orchard Cove, a strongbox of paper and coin, as a pyre for her worthless corpse? He treasured his pride. He jealously nurtured and protected it from all challengers, but at what price tonight? Would he sacrifice everything for a lifeless, white trash farm girl whose only worth was that she used to be the wife of Jagger Hill? Hell no! She wouldn't take from him in death what he wouldn't have conceded to her in life.

Slowly, almost imperceptibly, he lowered the pistol and stepped silently to the side. The old woman, eyes still blazing, slowly mounted the stairs with a massive negro attached to each of her arms, supplanting any weakness in her aged body. She was an unreckonable force as her flaming spirit fused to their frames as they strode up the steps with her and set about her work. Jagger had not even shaken himself from his stupor before the three emerged from the house with their prize. One of the men emerged first, carrying the small, limp contents of the coffin wrapped in a worn crazy quilt. The other man guided the old woman with one hand, and held a torch with the other. Her eyes no longer blazed but had returned to their milky blankness.

He thought at first that she would pass in silence, but at the last moment, she pulled herself free and announced like a prophetess, "We ain't done yet, Devil Man. We got her, but we done torn your house near up looking for that child. You done spirited him away somewhere tonight, and if we knowed for certain it wasn't to some hidden place in this hellhole, we would be dropping this torch before we leave this place. Our business with you be half done tonight, but not all the way done. As God above is my witness, that child don't belong to you, and he won't always be with you. You just keep yourself worrying about us, but we is the least of your worries. Devil Man, you got a worry that you don't know nothing about."

In silence, she descended the stairs, mounted the creaking seat of the buckboard beside Big John, and rocked back and forth on her perch as the mules ferried the passengers into the darkness. Jagger Hill watched the flickers of their orange torchlight until the wagon rounded the bend at the far end of the drive.

Quietly, he walked back in the house and closed the door. He straightened the furniture knocked over by the intruders. Rounding the doorway of the drawing room, he slowed his pace until he stood resolutely before the coffin, now empty except for two neglected gold pieces. Deftly, he returned them to his vest pocket. With his left hand, he reached up and pulled down the cover of the velvet-lined casket.

Speaking aloud in the empty room, Jagger pronounced, "My luck that they thought I knew where the boy was. He'll pay when I do find him, but there'll be time for that. More important details to attend to first. There will be no viewing of the body tomorrow. Word'll be sent in the morning that I've been overwhelmed with unbearable grief. The casket will be sealed and will lie in state in my church tomorrow. People in town will think me all the more admirable for loving with a love which wounds. Otherwise, plans will proceed on schedule. As soon as I get clear title to that farm, I'll take care of that crazy, old bitch."

With no further fanfare, Jagger Hill retired for the evening.

Chapter Twenty
The Peddler

The splintered seat bounced up and down beneath the skinny ass of Emile Dupont as the peddler's goods swayed on the eaves of his covered cart. He had long ago left the smooth dirt roads of what passed for civilization in these parts, and now he climbed the badly rutted paths of the high country. Huge hemlocks pressed in upon him, deepening the gloom that permeated the woods and his soul. One more farmstead and he could happily turn his traveling mercantile around for the brighter valley floor far below him. Emile attempted to spit from his parched mouth as he lashed the backside of his mule.

"Get up then, damn you." toned the Frenchmen. "And damn you too liberte, fraternite, and egalite," he shouted into the oppres-sive air of the dense forest.

Emile had fought in the wars of the Old World, and as a mercenary in the wars of the new. Completely disillusioned, he had simply ridden away from the battlefield, bartered his military artifacts for dry goods, and headed for the hills. If there was freedom to be found, it was in the solitude of the mountains, not in the company of humanity.

Occasionally, Emile would pull into town and quickly resupply his cart with food staples, lamp oil, tin ware, and tools. With the treasures and necessities of life in tow, he headed upward to the remote hollers of the mountains to peddle his wares at a substantial profit. This fueled his freedom on the open road. On this particular trip, he had made a potentially disastrous mistake. Leaving town, he encountered a farmer with a freshly fermented barrel of muscadine wine. Though a Frenchman would rather drink mud from a work boot than drink this purple swill, Emile had wrongly assumed that these hill people also thought of the pressings of the grape as a necessity of life. He had underestimated their ignorance. Every time he tried to unload some of the brew, he was showered with the scorn of Bible thumpers as they spewed invectives at him for his pagan ways. Now, the barrel weighed down his wagon and darkened his mood as its contents splashed back and forth in the oaken keg.

"I should just pull to the side of a bridge and feed this piss to unsuspecting fish below." fumed Emile. "I should let it run down the pilings like pee down the leg of an old man who cannot hold his water."

Dupont resisted the temptation and held out faint hope that his next customer might be a fool. The wagon jolted to a halt.

Cursing with a soup of French and ill-conceived English, the peddler dismounted the wagon seat, waded into the mud, put his shoulder to the wheel, and pushed. The cart rocked forward, but then back again. Emile had a tantrum, jumped to the side of the conveyance, and lashed the poor mule with all of his strength. Baring its huge teeth and shrieking in response, the animal lurched forward, freeing the cart. Sweating, Emile mounted the wagon seat and continued his assault on the mountain.

Within the hour, the peddler's eyes were blessed with the curls of white smoke rising from the last outposts of his journey. He wouldn't have put this much effort into the climb if the man in the cabin ahead had not been his best customer. Though young, he was a hermit who apparently prized his freedom and solitude even more than the peddler.

"Bonjour, my young friend!" shouted the Frenchman.

"Hello," called back Josiah Buckland. "Just in time for dinner."

Emile winced at Josiah's invitation. He knew what passed for a meal at this cabin. He craved some venison with fresh herbs, but he knew it was a fool's desire. As he dismounted the wagon, his nose crushed the last of his hopes. Emile's nostrils flared as they met the unmistakable stench of bear meat festering in its own fetid fat. Emile took an involuntary step backward as he cleared his senses with a whiff of a lavender-saturated handkerchief, which he kept in his pocket for just such occasions.

"Oh, too much the pity. I have just eaten," piped Emile. "Just time for a little business and talk before my return to the valley."

Though a man of few words, Josiah tried to hold up his end of the conversation as he handed the merchant his list and his money. Emile opened the flap at the back of the wagon and added the items to an old wooden packing crate. When finished, he handed the crate down to the young man. However, before crawling from the wagon he took a tin mug and drew off a cup of the wine. Passing the still frothy wine down to his unsuspecting customer, Emile bounded from the cart. When he straightened back to his full height, the mug was passed back to him.

"Sorry, Emile, no offense, but it just isn't time for this. Maybe some other time. So how has business been?"

The Frenchman once again was tempted to pour out the wine, but bad wine was still wine. Holding his nose, he gulped down the whole mug. Emile spat the remaining purple-tinged saliva from his mouth, but smiled involuntarily as he pondered the aftertaste.

"Maybe it is not so bad after all," he hummed. "Oh, business is good, so good it's been hard to get all of my food supplies. Big gathering up at the Orchard Cove with the death of Monsieur Hill's wife. Wiped out most of the flour and sugar in town."

As Emile turned to conduct his final business with Josiah, he was shocked by the young man's appearance. Josiah was silent and ashen-faced. Without uttering another word, he retreated to his cabin and slammed the door behind him.

"Damned rude hillbilly," fumed Emile. He drew another pint of wine, dropped the flap of his cart, and shook the reins of his mule for the descent to the valley below. Within hours and after several stops for re-fills, Emile found himself lonely and morose. The freedom of the open road was overrated. Though he satiated his desires with pleasure and escape, sometimes the loneliness was crushing. Distant rhythms of music revived his spirits. Peering from the side of his cart through the tangle of trees, he caught sight of a ramshackle building on a hill deep in the forest.

Chapter Twenty-One
The Road

Josiah's pulse quickened on his way down the hill, but he remained strong. The stark, gray framework of Vancie's old farmhouse shattered his soundness of mind. At that moment, everything trembled and fell. Like the banks of a muddy Southern river at flood stage, huge pieces of Josiah cracked, liquefied, and slid into the tumult of the flood. Collapsing from within, he suddenly felt his knees buckle and he fell into the earth of the last furlong to her house.

A cry pierced the air, more animal than human, as his scarecrow-like frame hit the greasy clay of the embankment. Pain seared through Josiah's heart like the blade of a knife taken from the flame and pressed to the raw flesh of a gaping wound. Time ceased to exist as Josiah's body writhed first in a gaping inaudible cry and then in convulsions of flesh. In a kaleidoscope of images, every memory of Vancie was unleashed like a primordial flood as he rolled about on the damp ground. The images of her haunting blue eyes and the redness of her lips hit him again and again. Never in all of his years in exile had he wished to die, but spinning through the blackness of these moments, Josiah wanted to die. To die of memory, longing, and loss. Josiah begged with all of his soul to the white afternoon clouds and blue sky that he might fall into forgetfulness of everything that it was to be mortal.

In his delirium, Josiah lost all perspective of his surroundings and convulsed with a start when a voice said, "We put her around back, Boy. We laid her out beneath that old hemlock to the back of the place."

The black furrowed face of Mattie, the Kellers' wash woman, loomed above Josiah and blocked the mocking brightness of the afternoon sun. From the wash sink in the kitchen, the old woman had seen the thin form of the mountain man lurch into view at the top of the hill. Mattie still knew him. She had never believed he ruined Vancie. Many times, in the swelter and glistening sheen of worship in her old wreck of a church, Mattie had heard Brother Andrew say, "Faith is being sure of what we hope for and certain of what we do not see. This is what the ancients were praised for..."

Mattie was an ancient. Her brown eyes had long since milked over, but an imperishable flame lived within them, by which she saw things unseen by younger eyes.

"Git up, Boy. Git your raggedy self up off of that ground, and go see to her. That poor gal done wasted all of her life away in this here world and part of her life in the other waiting to see you. Go show yourself to her."

Josiah rose up from the ground by a force not his own. Bone coming to bone and flesh to flesh, he rose up and crossed the last hundred yards around the corner of the house to the shaded space beneath the towering hemlock. Spirit failed flesh once again, and he fell through time. Hot tears scalded his cheeks, dripped salt into his mouth, and showered the earth. Only one word formed and passed over and over again from his lips into the shaded air beneath the tree.

"Vancie."

His gnarled, blistered hand reached out and wiped the dried grass from the name carved in granite beneath the palm of his hand. "Vancie."

"I said get yourself up. She had a boy."

Why did Mattie seem intent on twisting the knife in Josiah's heart by reminding him of the child that Vancie had with Jagger Hill?

"Why should I care about the boy? He has a father." Josiah asked bitterly.

"You're the boy's father." Mattie spat back at him.

Josiah froze in shock and disbelief.

"You're the boy's father, and unless I be wrong, your boy is in a whole lot of trouble." Mattie lifted her milky eyes toward an ever-darkening sky. "He's headed to the old church in the woods, but you need to head to the waterfall."

Chapter Twenty-Two
The Whipping

More than any other time, James dreaded dinner at Orchard Cove. Sometimes, he could get away with eating breakfast or lunch with the help at a kitchen table, but never dinner. Even though he and Jagger were now the only ones who dined at Orchard Cove, he was required to wash and dress for dinner. He sat at one end of the long, mahogany dining table, and Jagger at the other. Full complements of china serving dishes, crystal goblets, and sterling silver flatware closed some of the space between the two of them. Most evenings, they sat in candlelit silence as James listened to Jagger crunch the bones and suck the marrow from quail, chicken, duck, goose, cow, or occasionally deer. Vegetables, bread, fruit, and desserts were mandatory parts of every dinner, but they were an afterthought to Jagger. Most dinners were spent in silence, but James wasn't so lucky this evening.

Coolly, Jagger pulled a leg from the roasted chicken on the platter in front of him.

"Where were you this afternoon, Boy?"

James felt every fiber of his body tighten. Could his father possibly know that he had, in a moment of madness, violated the edict to stay out of the woods?

"I just walked downtown to buy some candy." James lied.

Silently, Jagger rose from the table.

"Then could you begin to tell me why Mr. Taylor, my land surveyor, told me that he saw you out on the Tryon Road?"

James felt his body grow numb and cold.

"Well…"

"Shut your damned mouth!" growled Jagger. He closed a little more of the distance between them. "You and I both know what's out the Tryon Road, and it's not a candy store."

James immediately understood that his mother no longer stood between the two of them to absorb Jagger's abuse. Jagger pounced like a puma. Imported china and crystal shattered in fragments around him, and silverware clattered as Jagger ripped his son from his chair and pinned him, stomach down, to its arm. Before he could utter a cry, Jagger jerked twice on the back of his trousers popping buttons, peeling down underwear, and exposing his bare buttocks.

James had no time to form thoughts of shame. Modesty was the least of his problems when he was in the grips of a madman. Jagger ripped his belt free from his own pants, and the narrow leather strap struck like a diamondback rattler across James's exposed backside. Time after time, it tore flesh and released small channels of blood. James cried out the first time, but after that, the mind-numbing pain produced only a gaping hole in his face, like a fish from which air but no sound emerged. It was a good thing that Jagger had him pinned by his neck to the chair, because James felt his flailing legs tense, weaken, and then dangle loosely from the side arm. There was no more pain. His brain ceased to process any sensation as Jagger released blow after blow. While he whipped the boy, words spewed from Jagger Hill's mouth.

"How dare you defy me, you little piece of shit! Don't think that being my seed will save you. You've always been like her. Fair-haired, weak, and a fucking dreamer. If I didn't think that I could beat her out of you, I would kill you right here."

Jagger stopped; not out of mercy, but from sheer exhaustion. Now, the only sound came from the dining room door, which slowly creaked closed as the help retreated to the kitchen. No one would save him. Jagger tossed his limp body to the floor and allowed James's blood to stain an expensive Persian rug. James lay paralyzed with pants and underpants around his knees. Jagger retreated to his sleeping quarters in silence.

For hours James lay on the floor, unable to move. Jagger had every reason to assume victory, but in those hours, James came to a stark realization. Jagger was right. His soul bubbled with the essence of his mother. He felt her in every fiber of his being. However, as hard as he tried, he couldn't find a single shred of Jagger Hill within him. How could a boy be only his mother and none of his father? As hard as James sought, he only found his mother and some mysterious, unnamable other. He wasn't Jagger Hill. As he lay on the floor, one other insane realization came to him. As soon as he could get up and walk, he was going back to that church because his mother was calling him there. If he bled out crawling on his belly to that building, then that was where he would die. He might have to use Jagger Hill's last name in public, but from this night forward, he would be James Keller.

Chapter Twenty-Three
Church Too

James limped slowly and painfully up the trail into the woods. He could feel small rivulets of blood trickling down the backs of his legs each time he established a new foothold and tensed his thigh muscles to step upward. His backside felt like it had been swiped by the claws of a puma, and the steeper the trail became, the fainter he grew.

"I know that I've only been here once before, but it didn't seem to take this long," he moaned.

Just when he thought that he would have to lie down on the trail and die, James heard the obscure but certain sound of music as he caught sight of the top of the church shanty on the ridge.

It wasn't a sound like the sonorous bellows of the organ at Green River or the lighter sound of a piano; this music was compiled entirely from the human voice. James had never heard such music. He wasn't even sure that it was beautiful, but as he drew closer, it became clear to him that the music was pure and raw. He lumbered through the dirt-swept yard of the dilapidated building, unaware of how many people might be inside. Whether a dozen or a thousand, people were hard to count when they were one. Whoever was inside of this church sang as one. Their words rose and fell, soared and crashed like the waves of the wild Atlantic. It came though the walls, through the news-paper-stuffed holes of broken windows, and rattled the doors hanging precariously on fra-gile, rusty hinges. Suddenly, what had seemed only sound changed to meaning as the words took root in his brain:

> *I am a poor wayfaring stranger a trailin through this world of woe,*
> *And there's no sickness, toil, or danger in that bright world to which I go,*
> *I'm going there to meet my Savior,*
> *I'm going there, no more to roam.*
> *I'm just a poor wayfaring stranger on the road to that bright world to which I go.*

Slowly, James mounted the steps, took the door by its handle, and stepped inside. He stepped from hearing a song into a song. Fifty or so people sat not straight-backed in pews, but in a circle. Right arms and left arms rose and fell in tomahawk fashion with the cadence of the music. Voices barked, croaked, shouted, and keened in a maelstrom of power, unity, and praise.

> *Come ye sinners, poor and needy,*
> *Weak and wounded, sick and sore,*
> *Jesus ready stands to save you, full of*
> *pity, love and power*
> *He is able, He is able, He is willing*
> *Doubt no more.*

The room spun about James as an usher pulled him into the center of the circle beside the resolute song leader whose right arm rose high above her head and then fell in perfect rhythm like an ax. James gasped as he recognized the first face in the room. Mattie stood like a lighthouse in the midst of crashing waves, her eyes beaming down upon the boy with a tenderness and compassion greater than James had known in a long time. Around him, words rose, swirled and fell:

> *There is a fountain filled with blood*
> *flowing from Emmanuel's veins*
> *Its blood can make the foulest clean,*
> *Its blood availed for me,*
> *Its blood availed for me-e-e,*
> *Its blood availed for me.*
> *Its blood can make the foulest clean,*
> *its blood availed for me.*

James no longer knew or cared if his own blood still flowed down the back of his legs. He no longer cared about Jagger Hill or Orchard Cove. As he swooned in a sea of sound and solace, James knew that Jagger Hill had never been a real father to him and that Orchard Cove was a house and not a home. Other faces emerged from the crowd: the great head of Big John; the red-nosed visage of the peddler, Emile DuPont; Phineus Coble, the odd little cripple man who had kept the livery; Delilah Hart, the pretty lady who lived in the boarding house downtown; and the pale, stricken face of his father's kitchen girl, Rosemary. These people never darkened the door of Green River and probably would have been thrown out in the yard if they tried. The music swelled louder and the room spun. Several people split off from the back rows, went to a side room, and returned to the center with basins of water and towels.

One by one, people stopped their singing long enough to go from the circle, remove their paper-patched brogans caked with mud, and expose their callused, arthritic, smelly feet to the coolness of spring water and the softness of the touch of bent-kneed apostles intent on washing away the soil and toil of the Earth. James was lifted up, placed in a straight-backed chair, and unshod. An ancient, bespectacled man looked up at him from bathing his feet as the music reached a crescendo.

> *This is my father's world*
> *And to my listening ear*
> *All nature sings,*
> *And round me rings,*
> *The music of the spheres.*
> *This is my father's world*
> *And let me ne'er forget*
> *For though the wrong seems oft so strong,*
> *He is the ruler yet.*

Never had James known such love, healing, tenderness, and release. Tears streamed down his face, but for the first time in his young life, they were tears of joy rather than sorrow. Rosemary pressed through the crowd, pushing a salt-tinged piece of the best bread he had ever tasted to his lips. An odd fellow followed her with a wooden cup. He poured a bracing brew of muscadine wine into his mouth.

He toned in a broken French accent, "These are the body and the blood, broken and shed for you."

Through the stinging astringent grape in his mouth and the blur of saltwater in his eyes, James noticed for the first time that the church had a balcony. Two people were sitting in it side-by-side. His eyes cleared, and with a piercing cry, James shouted, "Mother! Mama Lois!"

The child collapsed.

James fell through oblivion, swirling in images of the clapboard church, the vortex of song, and ghosts from the past. When he finally opened his eyes, he was out in the yard propped up on a quilt. He became aware of several things simultaneously. Much to his embarrassment, he knew that someone had doctored his backside. Streaks across his buttocks pulsed in soothing heat from some country poultice. Tree branches and inquisitive onlookers smiled down at him from above. But he became most aware that he was famished. James didn't ever recall being so hungry, and the aroma of freshly-baked cornbread and other mysterious foods almost made him cry. One of the faces staring down at him was Mattie.

"Hungry?" she asked.

"Starving," James replied.

"Well, we got a cure for that."

The other scents in the air were mysterious because they were beneath his father's standards. He was introduced to the staples of most poor black and white people in the South. Pots and pans bubbled to the brim with pinto beans, collard greens, and buttery cornbread. Instead of the usual fatback, at great sacrifice, one of the poor farmers offered a young shoat for the feast. The small pig had been cooked in a pit all night over hickory and oak, and washed over with vinegar and chopped red peppers from neighboring gardens. Since there wasn't nearly enough meat to serve fifty hungry farmers, tradesmen and their kin, the precious meat had been picked clean from every bone on the pig, head and all. It was then submerged in chunks in the boiling cauldrons to flavor the collards and beans with the essence of glistening, smoky, hot-spiced pork. The only other meat on the table was a grotesque platter of frog legs, but sides of mountain onions, pickles, and chow-chow filled the table, along with blackberry, blueberry, and damson cobblers. Huge crocks on each end of the table were filled to the brim with cold spring water and new apple cider chilled in the creek. On a table by itself off to the side, a wooden keg marked "Grown Ups Only" was getting a lot of use.

"Child, this is just an old poor man's supper. You ought to come on back and see us come fall when we has a real dinner on the grounds." rumbled Big John.

James didn't care what Big John called the spread. He didn't even care that he didn't know the name of half the food he was putting in his mouth. He just ate with wild abandon, waited upon by kind strangers who hugged his neck and filled his plate. Even Miss Delilah, who used to work in town, came over, drew James's cheek to her ample breasts, and told him what a fine man he would be some day. James noticed with great surprise that when she returned to her table, it was to a seat beside a beaming Mr. Coble. They seemed like an odd, but happy pair.

As he ate, glistening hog drippings coated his tongue. Sweet, melted butter slid with coarse, salty cornbread down his gullet. Tart, vinegar-coated greens, pungent spring onions, and sour blackberry juice joined in quick succession. Soon, the salt did its work, and James slaked his thirst with jar after jar of spring water and cider. Within the hour, James collapsed back on the quilt in a stupor of pleasure and misery. The misery had been brought on by his hedonism and the first fragmentary memories of his vision in the balcony.

Mattie saw the pain cloud his face.

"Lamb, you saw what you saw. Weren't no ghosts or no haints. Sometimes the curtain gets thin between this world and the other one. They ain't forgot you. He's never going to leave or forsake you. You can count on that."

Nothing in Jagger Hill's house had prepared him to count on that, but he found Mattie's words strangely comforting. James stretched out on the quilt and slept, but for the first time in a long while, he slept in peace.

Chapter Twenty-Four
Fire-Breathing Dragon

Rage burned within Josiah's chest as he took long strides down Black Rock Road toward town. He had no time or inclination to reflect on his first entrance to Tugaloo. That had been a thousand years ago, and he was now consumed by his obsession of settling an old score. For years now, all of his anger had been channeled into the hard labor of his exile in the high hills. He knew that Jagger Hill had not literally killed Vancie, but perhaps he'd done worse. From what little information he had, he knew that Jagger slowly tortured her through his actions and inactions, squeezing the will to live out of her until her spirit lifted from her body in despair. He thought about finding Jagger in his home and burning it to the ground, but even in his rage Josiah's moral core pulled him back from the abyss. He couldn't risk hurting others in his attempt to extract vengeance on Jagger, and he couldn't sacrifice his time in senseless acts of rage. It was a long way to Parson's Falls, and he was unsure how much time he had and what kind of trouble James might be in. Though Mattie saw more than most, even she didn't see all things.

Different routes to the falls flashed through Josiah's fevered brow, but none provided any particular advantage over another. He feared arriving at the falls in a state of exhaustion, but he feared arriving too late even more. As the morning waned, the miles ticked by until Josiah looked up and saw a larger and more chaotic Tugaloo. Gone were the ramshackle storefronts and mud-rutted streets. Josiah jostled through the noisy, crowded main street, astounded by gleaming buildings plastered with banners that trumpeted the obscene name of Jagger Hill.

The noonday train sat parked at the station for the firemen and engineers' lunch break. The iron behemoth crouched close to the tracks, spewing sprays of steam from each side of its massive head. Josiah stopped, surrounded by streams of strangers passing to and fro in manic procession. Steam not only billowed toward him, but he also felt a fire rising within him. If only he had an ax capable of putting the smallest dent in Jagger's train, he would break his own arms in the effort. The long rifle hanging from his right hand would obviously do the ironclad engine no harm. Sadly, there would be no slaying of this dragon with any weapon at his disposal.

Suddenly, an idea congealed in Josiah's mind, and a smile spread across his face. The mountains themselves might offered a weapon. He slipped past the distracted pedestrians, swung between the engine and fuel car, and mounted the side of the train. As he hoped, the small crew had all departed for the hotel for lunch. With no treasure on board, they had no need for a security detail to remain with the train. Josiah stared in great confusion at the dials and gauges before him. Had the train been headed upcountry, Josiah wouldn't have been able to move the beast, but it pointed downward toward Tryon. He only needed one control, and he soon found it.

With a strong jerk, Josiah released the brake on Jagger Hill's train. The passenger train had already passed through that morning, headed to Asheville, and there would be no obstructions on the tracks. The hulk of iron slowly pulled away from the platform. In a manner of minutes, it slipped through the edges of town with several wide-eyed citizens following in futile pursuit. Over the course of a few hundred yards, the train gained momentum. The wind whistled through Josiah's dampened hair as he threw shovel after shovel of coal into the flame-filled belly of the great serpent as it slithered around bend after bend.

It would soon arrive at the intersection of the train tracks with the Stairway to Heaven, an ancient Cherokee footpath. If his leap from the train didn't kill him, it would place him far closer to the falls and in a more rested state. For now, he reveled in the sweat and passion of feeding the beast. Flames leapt from the door of the boiler and steam enveloped Josiah as the train plunged down the hillside toward the edge of the escarpment. With a last jerk on the overhanging cord, the monster issued a blood-curdling scream.

Josiah lunged from the side of the train and tumbled end over end. His rifle flew into the surrounding brush. There was a roar and an explosion as the full coil of the train jumped the tracks at the escarpment's edge and plummeted into the abyss of the flatlands. Beyond the range of Josiah's vision, the train fragmented like a meteor into thousands of chunks of molten metal raining down the cliffs of the mountainside and igniting small brushfires. The terrain was too steep for human habitation, but reptiles retreated to their holes, woodland creatures to their burrows, and birds to the safety of the heavens. Josiah lay stunned for a few moments, his vengeance partially satiated. Slowly, he rose, searched for his gun, reclaimed it, and limped toward the falls.

Chapter Twenty-Five
Rendezvous

After the church supper ended, James picked his stepping stones carefully and made his way up the mossy bed of Colt Creek. The falls had been calling him since his first visit, and he knew this place held some special meaning for his mother. It challenged his imagination to picture his mother ducking rhododendron branches and crawling over downed logs. The louder the falls got, the more her spirit stirred within him. Ever since seeing her in the balcony of the church, he had racked his brain for other places that as Mattie had said, "the curtain might be thin." This might well be a snipe hunt, but just the sensation of being in the forest made James feel close to Vancie and satisfied his hatred for Jagger by defying him once again.

He knew that Jagger would be searching for him. James was on the run, living off of the kindness of church folk at the poor man's supper. Jagger nearly killed him the last time he saw him, and there was no way that he was going to tempt fate again by returning to Orchard Cove. James had burned all of his bridges behind him. He was just trying to lose Jagger on the trail long enough to double back to town at night and hop a train down to the piedmont or up to higher mountains. Anywhere would be better and safer than Tugaloo. However, before he left, he wanted to try and see his mother one more time. Although vivid, the memory of his mother in the balcony had faded a bit already. Just one more time and he wouldn't have to take Mattie's word for it; he would know that his experience was real.

Gnats and mosquitoes tormented him as he torturously proceeded up the creek, sweating and swatting at biting things seen and unseen. When he could no longer stand it, he finally caught his first glimpse of the falls. In the midday sun, the waters glistened with radiance as they tumbled over the top of the ridge. James forgot his miseries and steeled his courage for a steep climb up the rocky, precarious stairs leading to the top of the falls.

*****

Jagger Hill had never known such a state of rage. Slapping laurel branches right and left, he charged like a bull down the old, forgotten Cherokee trail to the top of Parson's Falls. Hardly anybody even remembered that this trail existed, and Jagger was counting on James coming to the falls by way of the creek bed. When that kitchen bitch, Rosemary, had

128

finally betrayed Vancie's oldest and best kept secret, Jagger thought that he might burst into flames. So, James was some piece of dirt shit woodland trash from a teenaged half-Indian. The irony of it tore him apart. Jagger couldn't believe that he had contaminated his table with the bastard son of a white trash farm girl and a hillbilly. He had forgiven the farm girl because of her beauty as breeding stock, but to think that she'd already been poked by that boy before he had his way with her enraged him. His only relief was that he had lived in shame for twelve years thinking that he had sired a pasty-faced, gray-eyed weakling. At least he'd escaped the greater shame that would have come if his "heir" ever reached manhood and inherited his hard-won fortune. There was still time. Not with the kitchen bitch, Rosemary, though. Imagine her thinking that he would make the same mistake all over again in return for her loose lips.

"Hell, no!" he boomed at her. "I don't care what you think I owe you. I never asked anything of you, Bitch."

The next mistress of Orchard Cove would come with papers from New York or Boston. His days of lying with mixed breed dogs were over. Even though the outing of James's secret had saved Jagger greater future embarrassment, he wasn't willing to take any chances with the boy. He hadn't worked for the last twelve years to become the laughing stock of Tugaloo. He could ship Rosemary out of town on the next train. Hell, with his investments in the railroad, he could even make a little money on her ticket. She had already provided a double yield. Not only had she told Vancie's secret, but also she had been hanging out at the nigger church in the woods. James had told her about his attraction to Parson's Falls. He might not be there, but it was a start. He would track him to hell if he had to. Rosemary was easily enough shed, but with James, it was personal and would require a personal solution.

Jagger reached down and tapped the butcher knife he'd retrieved from the kitchen on his way out of his house. On the way to the kitchen, he had passed his gun case with some of the finest rifles and handguns in the state inside. They wouldn't do. He knew who the boy was, but the boy still thought that Jagger was his father. He wanted to be close and see the look of betrayal in the bastard's eyes when he twisted the blade. Suddenly, Jagger teetered on his heels as he reached the end of the trail and stared down into the cascading waters of Colt Creek. He backed away from the edge and stooped down behind a large rock in a clump of hemlock trees. Huffing and puffing, he waited and hoped that this entire afternoon had not been a wild goose chase. After about an hour, he was rewarded for his efforts. James's head bobbed up and down as he rose and stooped beneath rhododendron branches making his way slowly up to the base of the falls. Within moments, his slight frame and blond head disappeared, and Jagger realized that James has started the ascent of the rock stairs beside the falls.

Chapter Twenty-Six
Pursuit

Josiah panted as he crashed through one obstacle and then another, working his way up Colt Creek. Mattie's words still rang in his ears.

"He is your boy. She named him James after your father."

He would never completely understand what made Vancie turn from him to Jagger Hill. He never knew the man. However, he had encountered him on the old plank sidewalk many years ago, and in spite of the man's finery, Josiah had felt the hair rise on the back of his neck. His father had taught him years ago that a man should trust his instincts. He didn't have to understand them, just trust them. If Mattie was right, James would never be completely safe until he got him out of Tugaloo and away from Jagger Hill.

He knew though that he couldn't put all of this off on Jagger. Even though he and Vancie had been attracted to each other at the falls and had even come to love each other, Josiah couldn't escape the sickening feeling that the two of them had sped up a clock that day that might have been far kinder to all involved if they had just waited. He and Vancie had loved each other, but so many of their decisions were motivated by fear rather than trust. They chose, and the only life they would ever know together in this world was the short, tragic one that they had lived. But maybe it wasn't too late for James. Josiah had no idea how he would convince him that a complete stranger was actually his father. First, though, he had to find the boy.

After the lead from Mattie, he had picked up James's trail hours ago, but it was hard to follow. The boy tread softly in the woods and had already proven his tenacity to the seasoned woodsman. Josiah, wasn't so lucky. He was leaving a great deal more evidence of his passing as he clipped branch after branch with his long deer rifle. The rifle made following the trail more difficult, but he learned his lesson long ago about going into the woods unprepared. Josiah had vague memories of the distance to the falls, but as he questioned himself, he was encouraged by the sound of falling water and his first glimpse of his destination. Josiah stopped in his tracks, frozen in joy and terror. He had just seen his first view of his son halfway up the fall stairs, but he also glimpsed Jagger Hill emerging from a hemlock thicket at the top of the ridge.

*****

Jagger could hear James's footfalls as he neared the top of the stairs. Hiding took no real effort; he simply stepped behind the largest of the hemlocks. James puffed and panted over the last fallen log onto level ground on the western side of the stream. Although the breeze was refreshing and the view dizzying, James had not climbed to the top of Parson's Falls for sightseeing. During the climb, he held his breath in anticipation of catching even a fleeting glimpse of his mother. His hope waned with each stair he climbed, and it completely collapsed when he pulled himself over the last obstacle at the top of the falls. He looked around in silence and then broke down in tears. Wave after wave of pent up sorrow racked his small body.

"Well, you are the girl that I always believed you to be." Jagger said as he stepped from behind the tree.

James froze in terror. He hadn't laid eyes on Jagger since Jagger beat James to death. Before James could move, Jagger had closed the small distance, grabbed James by the hair with his right hand, and wrapped his left arm under James's armpit and across his small torso. The attack forced him to the edge of the falls, facing downward into the ravine. The only thing that separated the two of them from falling to their deaths was the small ledge in front of them. James's heart beat like a drum as Jagger released the hold on his hair, whipped the butcher knife from his belt, and held it against James's throat.

Jagger pressed his hot, foul breath against James's ear and whispered, "Well, Father Abraham might not have had the guts to sacrifice his own son, but I am no cowering woman like him. You are bad seed, and it's time that your father cut his losses and started all over again. I came all the way up here today to slit your throat and remind you just what a piece of worthless shit you really are. No one will save you here."

James couldn't breathe with the knife up against his throat, and he knew that he was doomed. Glancing to his left, he saw what he had come to Parson's Falls to see. His mother stood on the top step of the falls. He knew that he would soon die and join her, but the sight of her stirred a last streak of resistance within his soul. With his free arm, he reached for his belt, retrieved his own straight-bladed knife, and plunged it into Jagger's thigh. Jagger howled like a wounded beast and dropped his own knife in pain. He flung James down onto the ledge. As his knife skittered over the falls, Jagger yelled with rage and pulled his right foot back to kick James into the ravine. He never brought the leg forward.

James heard a loud crack in the ravine below and felt a spatter across his upturned face. Jagger teetered for a moment with blood running down his face from a dark, gaping hole between his eyes. Then his body crumpled forward, catapulting him into the violent cataracts of Parson's Falls and nearly sweeping James over the edge with him. James dug his hands into the clefts of the rock and felt Jagger's body tumble over his own. He slowly backed away from the edge on his belly. By the time he was able to stand, another grown man loomed over his small, petrified body.

Mustering the courage to look up, he stammered, "Who are you?"

When Josiah looked down into the boys upturned eyes, he caught his breath. Vancie's eyes peered back at him. Not just her blue eyes, but the flecks of his own gray eyes scattered about the orbs.

"Son, I don't know how to tell you this. There's no reason that you would or should believe a complete stranger after all that you've been through, but I am your father."

James stared up blankly into the haunting eyes that looked down upon him. He should have laughed at the lunacy of what the stranger said to him, but his mother had told him to trust a man like the one above him.

"What's your name?" James asked.

"I am Josiah Buckland," the man answered.

James reached into his damp right pocket. He pulled out a small gold pocket watch. Josiah gasped when he recognized it.

"My mother told me when she gave this watch to me that it held a secret." James muttered.

With his index finger, he tripped a small latch on the dented edge of the watch, and the back panel sprang open. Etched inside of the back face of the watch were the letters: *V.K. and J.B.*

Epilogue

All the goodbyes had been said, and James and Josiah now stood by a canoe on Green River. Within moments, James would leave all that had been bright, fair, dark, and evil about Tugaloo.

James was eager to be going home to the high country with his father. Under other circumstances, it would break his heart to leave behind the place so closely connected to his mother, Mama Lois, Mattie, and his new church family in the woods. But as he watched Josiah step into the back of the canoe, he made his peace with leaving. James lightly followed him and pushed with the paddle at his father's command to launch the vessel into the flow of the stream.

As they floated downstream, James watched otters play along the banks, ducks fly past overhead, and innumerable turtles slip off of logs into the ever-flowing stream of life. The sun beat down upon them on the rare occasion that they slipped out from the huge arboreal canopy overhead. In the warmth and silence of the afternoon, James found himself growing drowsy and slowly leaned back against his father's chest and legs. To the young boy, Josiah smelled like the forest itself. Scents of mud, deer hide, trees, and river water soothed him as he slumbered in the cradle of his father.

He, his father, and the river became one as the boat yielded itself to the energy of dancing waters. He felt Josiah bend slightly and kiss his matted hair. Instinctively, he fingered the smooth, cool case of the watch in his pocket and invited the spirit of his mother to join them. After many hours, the canoe reached the last furlongs of Green River, and the river slowly widened to the open waters of Lake Pisgah. Suddenly, a cry punctured their peace from a promontory. Perched as erect as a corn stalk in the garden in summer, Mattie sat in the buckboard with Big John on the landing. If her sounds were words, James never heard them, but he saw her raise her cane high in final salute as he and Josiah slipped beyond the river into open waters. Although James only saw Mattie and Big John, he heard a sharp intake of air from his father. Years afterward, Josiah would tell him that he had seen the blond-haired love of his youth in the buckboard beside Mattie, and that his heart had opened as he took in the last of her that he was to have in this world.

The sun set as they entered the dazzling vast expanse of the lake, and James caught a flash on the top of the cliffs to his right. A great osprey dove from the clifftop, plummeting before them. Within seconds, the bird hit the surface of the water and showered them with spray. In a clumsy, methodical fashion it emerged from the water with a large, silver fish thrashing in its talons. Straining above the weight of its catch, the bird rose, and the red rays of the sun caught the wet flesh of the fish and set it ablaze with sparks of fire and gold.

About the Author

Dr. Jim Gulledge is the Director of Academic Support Services and Assistant Professor of Developmental Studies at Pfeiffer University located in the Village of Misenheimer in North Carolina. The passion of his academic life is a course that he teaches every other year on the works of C.S. Lewis and J.R.R. Tolkien. He holds a B.A. in Christian education from Pfeiffer College, an M.A. in English from Clemson University, and a D. Min. from Gordon-Conwell Theological Seminary in South Hamilton, Massachusetts. Jim and his wife, Linda, are the proud parents of four children: Megan, Adam, Jenna, and Gillian. Jim attends New London United Methodist Church. In his spare time, he explores the nearby Uwharrie Mountains and serves as *guardian ad litem* for abused and neglected children in his community.

9 781625 969170